LAURA AND THE RAILROAD BARON

A MONTANA WOMEN NOVELLA

NANCY PIRRI

First Printing: 2017

ISBN: 978-1-68046-654-6

Published by Satin Romance
An Imprint of Melange Books, LLC
White Bear Lake, MN 55110
www.satinromance.com

Published in the United States of America.

Cover Design by Caroline Andrus

CHAPTER 1

July 1886
South Central Montana
The Woodbury Ranch

"Nineteen-year-old women do not have guardians," Laura Elizabeth Woodbury huffed.

No wonder the ranch hands referred to her as 'Princess Sapphire', thought Matt Black, stretched out in the side chair across from her. If it hadn't been for the curve of her breasts, she could have been a child sitting behind the desk. He guessed her booted feet didn't quite touch the floor. Bright red spots of color appeared on her fair cheeks, her complexion delicate as a porcelain doll. But the steel beneath that refined surface showed in her ramrod straight spine.

"I am sorry, Miss Woodbury," the solicitor, Samuel Simpson, replied. "You *do* need a guardian. Your father was quite adamant that you wouldn't be able to run this ranch on your own. And Mr. Black is a capable man. Give him a chance, won't you?"

"But I had a perfectly capable foreman until Mr. Black decided to relieve him of his position. John Whitman was the best foreman we ever had."

Sitting beside the lawyer, Matt Black decided she was deliberately ignoring him by failing to ask why he had to be present at the reading of her father's will. Though they'd met before, the circumstances were certainly less amiable this time.

"He was…until he showed a little bit too much personal interest in you," Mr. Simpson said uncomfortably.

Matt had found her in the barn, dressed as she was now in buckskin pants and a man's shirt. More specifically, he'd found her in the clutching embrace of her foreman, apparently not struggling to get away. He wondered why a gently born and raised woman would allow a man such liberties.

Laura's father had been a life-long friend of Paul Hill, Matt's uncle. Hill, being too ill himself to perform the duties for his friend upon his recent demise, had relegated the job to his nephew. Matt owed much of his success in life as both a railroad and lumber baron to his uncle, so he'd willingly agreed to attend to Miss Woodbury's future while on business in Montana.

"There's no need to worry," Samuel said. "Mr. Black will be in charge until he finds a new foreman for you. He'll be staying here in one of the guest rooms until he's completed his business."

Laura sputtered, "There was nothing wrong with how John handled the foreman job."

Matt sighed. The man may have been an adequate foreman, but he had no business putting his hands on her. Which was exactly what Matt told him when he tossed the no-good off the ranch.

"Miss Woodbury, this portion of this discussion should be between you and me, not Mr. Simpson."

She turned an ice-blue gaze on Matt, one he guessed likely silenced most men … not him.

His father had passed away when he was but sixteen, leaving him with four younger sisters and his mother to care for. He'd become the 'man' of the house then and, quite frankly, his gentle mother couldn't handle her brood of strong-willed daughters. Soon, he found himself in the unenviable position of being guardian and disciplinarian. A week didn't go by when one of his sisters was planted over his knee for a plain old-fashioned whipping. Initially, he'd hated the chore, but eventually fell naturally into the dominant role, and in due time, the girls listened to him, and the discipline sessions grew farther apart. Now, as they were all married, they were their husbands' responsibility, thank God.

Looking at the cool exterior of Laura Woodbury, he decided she was no different than his sisters and suspected sooner than later she'd be over his knee. He smiled at the thought, thinking how different this would be from spanking his sisters, but he was the man for the job, and would exert his authority over her. Sinking back against the back of his chair he found himself delighting in the prospect.

Trying to reason with her, he said, "Your father only wanted you to be cared for. He wanted you protected. That duty and responsibility has fallen to me." He smiled. "I won't be staying forever, just until you're settled."

Matt had to wonder about the uncertainty crossing her face. She appeared to not believe a single word he said. Her uncertain expression changed to sadness, and he tried recalling what he'd said to make her so melancholy. Recalling his words about how much her father had wanted her cared for must be the reason.

"What do you mean by 'settled'? My father never said a word about any of this to me."

"Settled, Miss Woodbury, as in married." With her long, gold hair and pretty features, Matt had the feeling finding a suitable man to marry her wouldn't be difficult.

She gasped, then started coughing behind her hand, her eyes filling with tears.

"Are you all right?" Matt asked as he went to stand but settled back in his chair at her upraised palm.

She pulled a lace handkerchief from her shirt's breast pocket and wiped her eyes. "You can't be serious!"

"I most certainly am." Matt rose from his chair, stepped forward and planted his hands on the desk. When he leaned toward her, she sank back in her chair, cringing away from him. "You may choose your future husband, but I have final approval."

"What gives you the right to order me about?"

"As Mr. Simpson informed you, I'm your guardian and protector." He straightened up and folded his arms across his chest.

"More like my jailer," she muttered.

3

"No, you're wrong. Your life won't change a bit, but I have a duty to perform—a job to do. And, remember, this wasn't my idea, but your father's."

Matt returned to his chair. From the high color in her complexion, he knew she was furious with him. He hoped they wouldn't clash too often before he finally married her off, yet somehow, he guessed it would be inevitable. Laura Woodbury needed to learn that she was a woman meant to be cared for by a man. She was young and reminded him of his ex-wife, who'd been little more than a child bride herself when they married.

Women generally followed the natural order in life when led by a strong man with a gentle manner and good intentions. He hadn't risen so far in life due to his sternness, but because of his charm. Treating her with care would make her see the way of things. He frowned and thought, if that didn't work he'd resort to treating her the way he had his sisters when they were ill-behaved—over his knee for a bare-bottomed spanking.

"Uh, could we continue with the reading of your father's will, Miss Woodbury?" Mr. Simpson's voice sounded worried.

She waved a careless hand. "In a moment. I've another question for Mr. Black. How did you know my father? He never spoke of you."

"My uncle, Paul Hill, had been a life-long friend of your father."

Laura smiled. "Yes, I remember Mr. Hill, though it's been several years since I've seen him. How has he been?"

"Not well. Your father appointed him as your guardian. Due to illness, he isn't up to the task. In his stead, he asked me to step in. Since I had railroad business to attend to here in Montana, it was convenient."

"I see." She grimaced. "How nice that my guardianship is so convenient for you."

Damn. *Convenient.* He hadn't meant to put things quite so crassly.

"Is there anything else?" she asked her solicitor, giving Mr. Black the cold shoulder.

"What you've just heard is the extent of it," he replied, obviously trying to mollify her.

As Simpson's low-pitched voice continued, Matt found himself having difficulty concentrating on the conversation. Besides, the rest of the will

4

was standard fair. Miss Woodbury should have no other complaints. She'd been left, as Woodbury's only heir, an exceedingly wealthy woman.

Exhaustion overwhelmed him. His lack of sleep during his journey to Montana over the past week had finally caught up with him. Earlier in the day, he'd glimpsed the bed in the guest room and was looking forward to escaping into blissful slumber.

Laura's soft, melodic voice caught his attention. "That settles things, doesn't it?" She rose from her chair. Matt and Simpson rose as well. She shook Simpson's hand—much as a man would, Matt thought—then strode from the library, without saying a word to him.

He followed her, his gaze riveted to her plump, womanly bottom, her hips swinging alluringly as she left. It hadn't taken Matt long to realize Laura Woodbury had been allowed to wear the pants in her household far too long. That would stop immediately. No more wearing buckskin trousers as she'd worn today. With a bottom as fine as hers, a man could get the wrong impression about her. He sighed. Teaching her how to become a lady would be a major chore, but he guessed he'd be the only one she'd listen to for he'd give her no choice.

Simpson shook Matt's hand. "I warned you that Miss Woodbury was used to being in charge, didn't I?" he said dryly.

"You did. I've never met a woman quite like her," Matt said. Most women of his acquaintance would never want to take up the mantle of responsibility.

Simpson narrowed his eyes. "You admire her, don't you? I hear it in your voice."

"Yes, I do. If she has, in fact, been in charge of this ranch for the past several years, from all appearances she's done well by it."

Simpson picked up his satchel. "You know she'll object vehemently if you interfere with the ranch operations, don't you?"

Matt shoved his hands into his pockets and sighed. "I know. I will only interfere if I believe she's being endangered, or if the work is too difficult. Otherwise, I know little about ranching and will leave it up to her."

"Good luck to you, Black. Call me if you need my services."

"I shall and thank you."

On his way out of the library, Matt caught a glimpse of Laura's well-rounded rear at the top of the stair's landing.

He called out, "Miss Woodbury? Where are you off to?"

She peered down at him. "To change for dinner, of course."

Matt gave an approving nod. "Excellent idea. I'll meet you in the dining room shortly."

Satisfied, he strode down the hall to the dining room, confident Miss Woodbury understood how things would be between them.

"Mary! Please fetch me my mother's red satin gown. You'll find it at the very back of the closet."

"Your mother wore that gown for a costume party. 'Tis positively…"

"—indecent. I know," Laura said.

"You want to appear a whore in Mr. Black's eyes?" her maid asked, her Irish lilt still evident, though she'd lived in America for ten years.

"You may be the best maid I've ever had, Mary O'Garrity, but you won't be telling me how to dress, thank you very much. I won't appear cheap in the gown, just more grown up."

"No, ye won't, and I won't help ye make a fool of yourself."

Laura narrowed her eyes on Mary, who stood across from her, scowling.

"I'm going to prove a point this evening to my houseguest."

"What point would that be?" Mary said dryly.

"That I'm a full-grown woman and able to take care of myself, including selecting my own husband and making my own decisions."

Mary lifted one eyebrow. "I'd no idea ye were gettin' married."

"I'm not. I just have to convince Mr. Black of the fact that—when and if I do decide to marry—it'll be to a man of my own choosing. Mr. Black *claims* I may choose my own husband, with his final approval, of course, but I don't believe a word he says. Oh, how could my father put that man in charge of me?"

"What in heavens are ye talkin' about?"

"Mr. Black, by proxy, has been appointed my guardian. Father's last will states that a suitable man must be found to marry me."

Mary sighed. "Ye know, your father spoiled ye. Now that he's gone on to meet his Maker, he's left ye in the hands of a man who won't allow ye to have the upper hand. 'Tis the smartest thing he's ever done, in my opinion."

"Mary! How can you even think that?"

"'Tis the truth."

"Haven't I kept this ranch running smoothly?"

"You've done a superior job, Miss Laura, but now 'tis time to take the place the Almighty meant for ye to take."

Oh, she hated when Mary spoke this way; hated how society believed it not normal for a woman to wear pants and to manage her own life. Every Sunday, without fail, Pastor Porter did nothing but lecture about a woman's place in life, looking directly at her the entire time.

She thought about Mary's comment regarding her father spoiling her. He *had* spoiled her—until her brother, Jeremy's death. Then he'd quite simply ignored her. No longer was she his beloved Princess Sapphire. Painful memories of sitting, night after night at the dinner table with him, made her heart clench in agony. Shunned, utterly and completely, he'd removed her from his life, speaking little to her, barely noticing her presence. Frankly, she'd been amazed he'd kept her in his will, but then he'd had no one else.

Mary pulled the gown from the closet and carried it to Laura's bed. As Mary tightened her corset, Laura sighed at her maid's disapproving expression. Once Laura donned the gown, she stared at her reflection in the full-length mirror. The vivid red gown had been fashioned of satin with a plunging rounded neckline, exposing the moon crescent tops of her breasts. The gown was more risqué then she recalled. The waistline was tight over her corset, the skirt slim and fitted, the hem of the skirt billowing into a slight train.

She stumbled, managing to catch herself upon entering the dining room. Mr. Black's initial welcoming smile abruptly disappeared upon her entrance. He scowled as he rose from his seat at the end of the table and strode toward her. His crisp white shirt, black tie, and broad shoulders clad in a fine black, lightweight serge jacket made Laura aware of his male attributes. His raven-colored hair was cut a bit long and reached his collar and contrasted starkly with his steel gray eyes.

Laura decided his dark, brooding masculinity likely appealed to many women, but not her. She much preferred John's fairness and soft spoken, gentlemanly manners. Mr. Black, on the other hand, had been nothing but dictatorial toward her. Though not ungentlemanly, she grudgingly admitted.

Before John had been booted off the ranch, she believed he had been on the verge of asking to court her—his kiss told her so. Perhaps, if he hadn't yet left town, she'd ask him how he felt about her. Oh, she knew most women would play the game for months, or even years, but she didn't have the luxury of time. According to her new guardian, she was on the marriage block, and, though he hadn't said it, she guessed he meant to rid himself of his new responsibility as quickly as possible.

She lost a bit of her confidence when she saw the smoldering look in Mr. Black's eyes from where he now stood beside her chair. While she had no desire to start a row with the man, she had no intention of changing out of the risqué gown. Smugly, she felt sure Mr. Black would soon understand she was an independent woman. No one told her how to live her life.

He held her chair for her, and she sank into it. Chills ran up over her bosom and down her bare arms, his big body seemingly surrounding her as he solicitously pushed her chair up to the table. She felt superior strength in that push. Unwillingly, she compared John's narrow frame to Black's sturdy build, recalling how weak John's arms had felt around her.

Mr. Black returned to his own seat, and Laura breathed a relieved sigh. Mildred Hanson, the cook, appeared and served them each a bowl of creamy potato soup. The woman's chatter grated on Laura's nerves, but her guest seemed to enjoy it and engaged Mildred in pleasant conversation. After the older woman left, Laura glanced at him. The scowl had reappeared, and he met her eyes.

"I see you've dressed for dinner."

His casual comment on her appearance startled her momentarily, but she murmured, "Father and I have always done so."

Her cheeks felt hot, and Laura knew they were flushed. Lord, why had she done such a silly thing as to wear this gown? Mr. Black appeared ready to … Well, if she didn't know better, she'd think him ready to throttle her.

He waved his fork toward her, his gaze on her breasts. "I realize this is the hot season, but you may want to cover up a bit next time."

CHAPTER 2

*L*aura had just lifted her spoon to her lips when she set it down. Her voice trembled when she replied, "You can't dictate to me how to dress."

"Someone must, since you've abysmal taste in clothing," he remarked. "I'll examine your wardrobe tomorrow and toss out what I believe are unsuitable garments for a young woman of your age and station."

Rising from her seat, she said, "I beg your pardon?"

One eyebrow lifted. "I see I'll have to call upon a doctor to see about your hearing problem as well."

Lifting her chin, she said coolly, "I won't tolerate you going through my belongings. You'll stay out of my room, and you won't make any decisions regarding my manner of dress." She looked down at her gown, then met his eyes once more. "As you can see, I'm a woman, full-grown. Now, then, if you'll excuse me, I've lost my appetite." She took a step away from the table.

"Sit down, Miss Woodbury," he ordered.

Laura paused when she heard the soft, yet steely tone in his voice. She whirled to face him and met his dark, intent look.

"We haven't finished this conversation. Sit down and eat. After dinner, we'll come to an understanding."

Laura turned away in complete defiance just as Mildred reappeared, platters of food in her hands.

"Oh, you can't be done eating yet, Miss Laura!" she exclaimed. "You haven't even finished your soup."

"As I've just informed Mr. Black, I've no appetite this evening. I'm going for a ride and will return later."

"Absolutely not," Matt declared.

The cook gasped and set down the plates, one at Laura's place, and the other in front of Matt. Lifting her skirt, she scuttled into the kitchen.

Laura jammed her hands on her hips. "I always ride after supper," she informed him.

He rose and tossed down his snowy napkin. "Aside from the fact you've refused to eat, riding alone in the evening is inappropriate for a young woman, not to mention dangerous, be she ever so mature."

When he headed toward her, she started backing away. "I'm going riding, and you will not stop me."

Whirling away from him, she heard him at her heels and knew she wasn't quick enough. His hands grasped her arms from behind. He held her in place and spoke softly in her ear, his breath and words ruffling her hair. "Go to your room."

The contact from his big, warm hands on her arms made her realize his strength once more, though his touch was gentle. Laura pulled out of his grasp and faced him. "How dare you touch me!"

"I haven't begun to touch you in the way you deserve, young lady."

"What!" she gasped. "You mean to ra—"

"Not *that*," he growled. "Young women that behave like spoiled brats require a trip over the knee for a well-deserved spanking."

Laura gasped in outrage, not only at his words, but in the steely look of determination on his face. She felt tears of fury fill her eyes and prayed they wouldn't seep out. While she wanted to defy him, she decided it might be unwise. She knew some men took delight in hurting women to get their way. She'd overheard gossip from one of her maids that John might have been such a man, though he'd never behaved that way with her.

She wouldn't put it past this determined man from doing exactly as he threatened, still, it was difficult to be obedient. No man had ever given her orders—ridiculous ones at that. Not even her father had treated her like a child.

Laura glared at Matt, daring him to do his worst. "I can't believe you'd even try to … discipline me," she spat.

"Oh, I dare, and much more, if you don't behave." He pointed his finger toward the stairs.

She bit her lip so hard she felt the metallic taste of blood. Her plan had, obviously, back-fired on her. Why hadn't she listened to Mary?

With as much decorum as she could muster, she lifted her chin and made her way, nearly running across the hall and up the stairs. She recalled the tingling sensations rushing up and down her spine when he'd touched her, a sensation that had been far from unpleasant. What was wrong with her? She'd stood close to men before—while dancing. She'd been touched before, including being held in John Whitman's arms. But never had she felt this sort of awareness, starting at the top of her head to the very soles of her feet. And, in her center, her heart pounded briskly in acknowledgement of Matt Black's unquestionable masculinity.

As soon as she entered her room, she closed the door and flung herself down on the bed. She felt discouraged and was thoroughly disgusted that she'd obeyed Mr. Black. But then she truly didn't know him, or of what he was capable. A spanking! The nerve of the man, she mused, even as heat rushed through her body, imagining him flinging her over his lap, raising her skirts, and— She cringed and squeezed her eyes shut.

Then she thought of John again. His gentle smile spoke of the possibility of intimacy. She guessed his fair hair and soulful brown eyes would melt any woman's heart. She just knew he would be a tender man. Never would she believe he'd harm her or lay a hand on her.

Tomorrow she'd travel into Bozeman to see if John had left. If he hadn't, she'd hire him back. She knew Mr. Black wouldn't approve of her seeing John, and he definitely wouldn't want her offering him his job back, especially since he'd fired him in the first place. But she'd had her sights set on John since the moment she'd convinced her father to hire him. Thinking of her reasons for hiring John back, though, she admitted retaliation against Mr. Black seemed to be the primary one.

She undressed and pulled on her nightshift. After tossing and turning for several hours, she knew she'd never fall asleep unless she took a ride. The grandfather clock in the downstairs hallway chimed the hour of midnight. She dressed in her shirt and buckskins again, then tugged on her leather boots. She had a feeling John was still in town, likely down at Shorty's Saloon, with his friends.

Reaching up, she pulled her hat from a shelf inside her armoire, left her room, took the iron key from her pocket and locked her door before making her way down the stairs. Just as she approached the library, she saw a light shining from beneath the door. Darn! He hadn't gone to bed yet. Closing her eyes, she took a few deep breaths, deciding it was now or never before slipping past the closed door and out of the house.

*att trudged up the stairs at half past midnight, having had to meet with the cook before settling down for a long awaited rest. He reached the landing, noted Laura's closed door further down the hall, and was satisfied she'd obeyed him. Just outside his room, he paused. Something gnawed at him—something wasn't right. Laura had been adamant about riding. He wasn't stupid enough to believe she would meekly obey him, so he turned and walked down the hallway, stopping outside her door.

His hand covered the doorknob. He tried turning it but found it locked. No surprise there, seeing as how he knew he hadn't made much of an impression on Miss Laura, except to cow her. He wondered if he'd even managed that. Her father had given her far too many liberties, but then he'd been a tired old man. Maybe he was entitled to spoil his only child, a child he'd raised alone for most of her life. Matt wasn't old at twenty-eight, just tired and skeptical at the moment about his ability to deal with the feisty Miss Laura.

Was she actually behind this locked door? Somehow, he doubted it. He tore down the stairs and out the front door. At the barn, he found Laura's groom sound asleep in a stall. Matt shook the boy's shoulder.

He sat up in confusion, rubbed his eyes, then stumbled over his feet as he tried to stand.

"Where is she?" Matt bit out.

"Went—she went for a ride, sir," the boy stuttered. "Toward town."

"My God!" Matt exploded. "You'd better count on her being safe or you'll pay a heavy price. Next time, you ask permission of *me* first regarding Miss Laura's requests. Understand?"

The frightened boy nodded, then saddled the fastest horse in the stable. Matt leaned over the horse's neck and sped down the road toward town. Why was she headed there? Surely not in search of that bastard foreman. Matt rode faster.

By the time he reached Bozeman, it was after one o'clock and anger surged through him. He required sleep, not storming after this disobedient little wench under his guard.

The town still bustled with activity. He scoured Bozeman but found no sign of Laura. She'd likely just gone for a ride and was now safe and sound asleep in her bed, he decided, wondering how he'd missed not passing her on the road when he heard a man's soft-spoken voice followed by a girl's giggling. Frowning, he moved in that direction. Plastering himself against a building, he leaned forward and peered around the corner.

In the darkness, it was difficult to identify the individuals, but he smelled Laura before he saw her, her lavender scent permeating the air. He stepped away from the wall and managed to make out the small shape of his ward leaning close against a man's body. Then he saw the man take her hand in his. Matt's world turned red as he tore into the alley. He was astonished to see that, beneath the silvery moon's rays, it was John Whitcomb. Apparently, the man hadn't learned his lesson.

He yanked them apart and pulled his arm back.

"Mr. Black, don't!" Laura protested.

Matt smashed a fist into Whitman's gut, then delivered a right uppercut to his jaw. Whitman collapsed to the ground. Matt stared down at the unmoving man, then swiped an errant lock of hair back from his forehead and turned to Laura.

She stood ramrod straight, her hands on her hips. "Just what do you think you're doing?"

Matt heard the trembling fury in her voice.

From inside a saloon, he heard tinny music and a woman singing off-key. No one had heard the scuffle, which infuriated him further. If he hadn't arrived in time, there was no telling what Whitman would have done to her.

"Damn, saving your virtue. Apparently, you didn't want to be saved. Do you know you scared the ever-living hell out of me, leaving the ranch the way you did?" He stepped close and scowled down at her. "Why did you leave? To prove you don't have to follow my orders when you know I'm only doing what your father wanted?"

A mulish expression crossed Laura's face. "I wanted John back. Whatever else might be said about him, he was a more-than-adequate foreman. Even my father approved of him. And I always ride after supper. You've ruined everything. I offered John back his job, but now I'm certain he won't return to the ranch."

"You got that right, Miss Laura," John said.

Matt scowled down at the felled man.

John awkwardly rose and looked at Laura. "I hadn't gotten around to telling you, but I took a job at Stanton Smith's place." He reached down, picked up his hat from the ground and placed it on his head. His fingers touched the brim in salute to her. "Good luck, Miss Laura."

"Darn it," she muttered, scowling at Matt. "Now see what you've done? He's taken another job."

Matt watched the man limp away, damning himself for being so impetuous—something he rarely was, unless it had to do with Laura. This did not sit well with him. But then he thought of her in John's arms in the barn the day he'd arrived and decided he had been right to intervene.

He looked away, grimacing when he noticed for the first time the stench in the alleyway. "Let's get out of here," he muttered, deciding they'd finish the discussion tomorrow.

He gave her a leg up onto her mare. As they rode side by side out of town, they were silent for a long while. Finally, Matt spoke. "What am I going to do with you?"

"I am too old to be spanked."

"Hardly," he scoffed. "Since you're resistant to the idea though, what have you in mind, instead? You deserve punishment."

"Why, I suppose you could banish me to my room or put me on rations of bread and water. But I'll inform you now, I'd not stay put. Besides, Mildred would never let anyone starve."

Matt smiled. Then he tossed his head back and laughed. "That's hardly a practical measure. The one I'll implement will make a deeper impression on you, I believe."

"What would that be?"

He caught the hesitancy in her voice and sighed. He had no desire to hear her complaints but knew she'd badger him all the way home if he didn't explain her fate.

"Tomorrow you'll report to me early in the morning for a list of chores to complete."

"Oh. Is that all?"

"I'm not speaking of outdoor ranch work, which I know you enjoy and wouldn't be a punishment at all. No, you'll stay inside and work along with your maid. You will also give your cook a week off from working in your kitchen, paid, of course, and you'll cook the meals yourself."

She stopped her horse. "Now, just a minute—"

CHAPTER 3

$\mathcal{M}$att waited for the tirade to begin.

After a long pause, she said, "I'll handle the cooking. Cook's needed time off for ages."

Good grief. Matt hadn't expected her to be agreeable about his idea, but then he decided time would tell. Her cheery attitude would likely change once she'd put in a day or two of mundane, grueling housework.

He wouldn't allow her to work and dress like a man any longer, especially if he wanted to marry her off quickly. Then he thought, even dressed as a man, she had no trouble garnishing the interest of men. He also grudgingly admitted seeing her dressed in buckskins was enticing and seemed only to accentuate her womanly curves.

The rest of the ride home was accomplished in silence. The young groom ran out of the barn as soon as they arrived, a lantern in each hand. Matt dismounted quickly and hurried to assist Laura out of the saddle, only to find she'd already jumped down.

He came to a decision. "Tomorrow morning, after you've completed the assigned chores, come to the library. I'd like to discuss a few things with you."

She'd taken a lantern from the groom, then started for the house. "Keep

16

up with me if you want to be able to find your way inside," she threw over her shoulder.

Matt's long strides easily followed her until they reached the house. She opened the front door at the same time he did. His hand landed on top of hers for an instant. Releasing her hand, though he felt strangely reluctant to do so, he said, "Do you always open doors for yourself?"

Laura's brow lifted. "Why, I suppose I do. Is there a reason I shouldn't?"

"It's courteous and customary that a man open doors for a lady. Haven't you ever been courted?"

She bit her lower lip thoughtfully a moment before saying, "If you count the neighboring men folk stopping by for a glass of lemonade after work."

"That's not courting. That's being neighborly. All right, then that will be where we begin. I'll instruct you in what to expect and how to behave when a man comes courting."

She rolled her eyes at him. "If I must."

He found himself holding his breath as he stared down into her eyes. Matt had a feeling this woman had the ability to make a man feel … well, manly and protective—even dressed as a boy.

"Is there anything else?" she said. "I'm exhausted."

Gruffly, he replied, "Go on to bed. We'll talk in the morning."

"Excellent idea. Good night."

"Yes, good night," he murmured, heat seeping into his face when he found his gaze riveted on her well-rounded rear as she left him. He headed for the library. From a desk drawer, he found a piece of paper and pulled the fountain pen from its stand. He thought about his sisters and their charming ways. What could he teach Laura in regard to the feminine arts?

He started to write, but each idea of what to teach Laura that came from his pen met with him scribbling over it. Finally, he set the pen back in its place. It was useless. Even wearing pants, Laura Woodbury was femininity personified.

She didn't require lessons of any kind, especially from him. Still, he couldn't help but wonder why she favored men's trousers, and why she enjoyed pursuing men's work.

Then an unexpected thought came to mind. Perhaps she needed motherly tasks to bring the femininity he knew that lurked inside her to the surface. And then his son came to mind. He thought, perhaps, he should mention to Laura he had a son, whom he missed immensely, having left him with his parents in Minnesota. Still, he considered the idea of having him come out to Montana to be with him, then set the idea aside, guessing he wouldn't be here long, for Laura was lovely and would likely court and marry in the near future.

He came to his feet. Restlessly, he wandered around the library, pausing before the fireplace. On the mantle were several photographs. He recognized Laura, in varying stages of growth. He smiled, noting her petite size in youth had lingered into adulthood.

His gaze stalled on the next picture grouping, which included several photographs of a young man with hair the same golden color and eyes of blue like Laura's. The resemblance between them was astonishing. For certain they were related, but then he frowned. She was her father's only heir—his only child. Perhaps it hadn't always been that way though.

One of his passions in life was dissembling mysteries. Identifying this boy became important to him. Matt moved along the bookshelves, perusing the titles, searching for something that would give him a clue to his identity. He'd nearly given up when he saw a leather-bound book. Reaching up, he placed the Woodbury family Bible on the desk, sat down and began to look through the pages.

It was nearly two o'clock by the time Matt had what he believed was a clue to Laura's unorthodox behavior. Treading quietly upstairs to his bed, he slipped beneath the covers, exhausted. It felt strange lying down without first having said 'good-night' to his son, Jonathan. They had rarely been separated, and most trips Matt took Jonathan with him. But not this time as Matt had been uncertain about his responsibilities toward Miss Woodbury.

Exhaustion finally overtook him, and he slept.

———

*T*he sun was just beginning to peek above the horizon when Laura wakened the next morning. She'd had difficulty sleeping, waking off and on through the night, until a horse's neighing and voices pulled her from her slumber.

It was only five o'clock, and already her room felt hot and muggy. Still, she shrugged a robe on over her nightgown and moved to the window that overlooked the backyard. Several of her ranch hands had arrived, having traveled from their homes in town. They were ready to head out to various pastures to work. One young man, then another, noticed Laura looking down from her window. Paul, the younger of the two, waved and said, "How do, ma'am!"

Grinning, Laura waved back. "Morning, Peter, Jim. Looks like it'll be a clear day but hotter than Hades, doesn't it?"

"Yes, ma'am," they said in unison.

"Make sure you wear your hats, and take plenty of water," she said. "And finish early so you won't be out scorching in the heat of the day."

The Swede, as he was called, Gary Hanson, sidled up beside the other men. "You comin', Miss Laura?"

"No. Not today." She heard a door slam. Mr. Black appeared, having just exited the house. He tipped his hat to the men with a "Good morning" and moved toward the corral. He hadn't noticed her in the window.

The men left then, their horses kicking up dust as they rode down the road.

Charlie, her groom, was pulling on the lead of one of her new stallions. He'd bridled the horse, for what purpose she had no idea. She'd given strict orders to leave the animal in the pasture to run wild until she was ready to train him.

Mr. Black paused a short distance away from the boy and beast. She couldn't hear his words but saw his lips moving. She also saw how the beast's ears pricked up, his big, rolling eyes riveted on her guardian.

Moving closer, he reached out and took the lead from Charlie. With a gentle tug, the horse followed him into a corral close to the house. Laura leaned down and set her elbows on the ledge, watching him through the wide-open window. *What was the man about, anyway?*

He started leading the horse around the corral's perimeter. At one point, the animal reared up, but Mr. Black turned and faced him, his gentle, unthreatening demeanor immediately calming the horse. She realized then he was no stranger to horses. She liked that. Liked that a lot...which didn't sit well with her. She didn't want to like this controlling man who'd entered her life. *Whatever were you thinking, Father?* But then she remembered Mr. Black's uncle had actually been named her guardian. When he was unable to fulfill the duties required, Mr. Black was obliged to step in.

When the horse reared up again, nearly striking Mr. Black, she gasped and straightened up from her bent position at the window. Donning a pair of dungarees, long-sleeved shirt and boots, Laura tore down the stairs and ran outside. She halted upon reaching the corral.

Mr. Black stood in the center, lead in hand, clicking his tongue, encouraging the horse to pick up his pace as he ran briskly around the corral's perimeter. Laura admired the man's tall muscular body; his long legs he'd spread wide for balance, clad in tapered serge pants. His coat he'd left unbuttoned over a plain but crisp white shirt. Didn't he own any informal clothing?

He saw her and flashed a wide grin. "Good morning."

"'Morning," she murmured, relaxing against the fence, though inside her body her chest felt heavy, her heart doing somersaults. What an incredibly handsome, charming man—dangerously so, she mused. She focused on his tall, strong body, his intent, flinty-eyed look trained on the horse. She tore away from her wayward thoughts of how it might feel to kiss Mr. Black and watched him work the horse. After a while, she said, "I'm going to make some coffee. Want some?"

"Yes, thank you. You'll be preparing it, not your cook," he reminded her.

"Cook's not here, so how could I forget?" Turning on her heel, she walked swiftly to the house. Did he think she'd never done household chores before? Her father had always had a housekeeper, maids and a cook. Nevertheless, he'd insisted she learn to perform household chores, things he believed she would need in her future once she married. He'd always said, 'Unless you walk in the cook's or maid's shoes, you won't know how to supervise them.'

In the kitchen, she poured hot water over the coffee grounds in the pot, then set it on the burner as memories of her twin brother, Jeremy, flooded her. She recalled how jealous of him she'd been the year they turned twelve. He'd been allowed to work outside, alongside their father and the hands, while she'd been stuck inside performing women's work. She knew she wouldn't have minded if her mother had been alive to provide company, but she'd passed away shortly after giving birth to her and Jeremy.

Once the coffee was ready and piping hot, she carried two cups outside, setting one down on a corral post. She took a careful sip and sighed with pleasure at the strong taste of the brew. Looking up, she choked on her coffee when she saw Mr. Black sitting on the horse, bare-backed. She knew better than to make a sound for fear of spooking the animal. She stayed calm and took deep breaths, expecting the horse to toss him to the ground any moment.

He sat there, leaning over the animal's neck, stroking him and talking softly. She couldn't help but wonder at his words. Resentment filled her. She'd tried twice to mount this horse she had yet to name, with no success.

Matt slid from the animal's back, dropped the lead and strode toward her.

Laura picked up the cup she'd set down on the post and handed it to him. His hand brushed hers when he took it. She backed up a step even as quivers of unwanted desire ignited inside her. His touch made her feel all the things a woman felt for a man to whom she was attracted.

"What are your plans for the day?" she asked, deciding it would be good to know the whereabouts of her charming adversary.

One dark eyebrow lifted, and a slow smile tilted up his lips. "I'm walking the line, so I won't be back until after dark."

Laura breathed a deep, relieved sigh. She had plans to join some of her hands to help repair the corral at the west end of the property.

His next words made her think he was a mind reader. "Inside work today, only," he reminded her.

"I know."

She felt too tired to fight him. As a matter of fact, she would enjoy her day indoors—which, unknown to Matt, would be a welcome change. She swept a loose lock of hair back from her forehead, then sipped her coffee. Finally, she looked at him. "You're not a stranger to horseflesh."

Matt laughed. "It wasn't all that long ago my family owned a farm in southern Minnesota. We had lots of animals."

"Hmm, you have the appearance of someone raised in town. I'd assumed you'd have a fine carriage or two pulled by horses and wouldn't think to

21

ride one. You're good with them." Tilting her head to one side, she gave him a faint smile. "Think you'll be able to train this one?"

"No doubt in my mind, and within the next few days. I plan on using him as my main means of transportation while I'm here, if that's all right with you."

"I've no problem with that—if you can get him to mind. He seems to have a strong will of his own."

"Really?" He grinned. "I thought him rather docile."

Laura gave an unladylike snort by way of a reply.

"Have you eaten breakfast yet?" he asked.

"I'm just about to make ham and eggs and biscuits."

"You are?"

Scowling at him, she said, "Contrary to what you believe, I'm no stranger to household work." She took a last sip of her coffee. "What did you mean earlier when you said you'd be walking the line?"

He took her arm with one hand, held his coffee cup with the other and escorted her back to the house. "I'm here to supervise a crew of railroad men who are in the process of fixing broken track in this territory. Walking the line means the railroad track."

"I see. My solicitor said you were here to take care of me and my future."

"That, too," he said.

They entered the house. Laura made her way to the kitchen, aware of him close at her heels. She would have rather prepared the food without his observing her every move, but she knew he wouldn't leave her. An idea for keeping him focused on something other than what she was doing came to mind. "Excuse me a minute," she said.

In the library, she found a newspaper she'd picked up in town last week and carried it into the kitchen. She handed it to him.

He looked at her, raising his eyebrows as he took the paper. "Thank you."

Laura knew he was wondering why she was being so cooperative after her initial negative reaction to him showing up on her doorstep. Wondered why she was cooking and waiting on him. Heavens, if she wasn't careful, he'd expect her to retrieve his slippers for him! And, if she had to, she would, especially if it meant him leaving sooner rather than later.

Truthfully, she enjoyed cooking. Even the dusting didn't bother her. She enjoyed the respite from the back-breaking outdoor work, knowing soon she'd have to return to it. Her ranch hands needed her lead and direction. And she knew she would need to hire a new foreman.

Quickly, efficiently, she whipped up the biscuit batter, rolled and cut out perfectly round biscuits with a jar lid. She set them on the oven stone and slid them into the oven. Then she scrambled the eggs and grilled the ham slices in a pan. She left the food on the back burner, turned to Matt and said, "Do you mind if we eat here in the kitchen instead of the dining room? It'll be simpler."

"Fine with me."

She set the table while she waited for the biscuits to bake.

All the while, Matt sat seemingly engrossed in the paper.

Soon breakfast was ready. They sat across from each other, eating in silence. After his second helping, he looked up and gave her a long, steady look. "You're an excellent cook, Miss Laura."

Heat seeped into Laura's cheeks, not because of his words of appreciation but because of the admiration in his eyes. "Thank you," she murmured as she rose, picked up her plate and silverware and made her way to the sink.

Matt chuckled. She peered at him over her shoulder. "What's so funny?"

He sank back in his chair, his laughter subsiding. She turned hot then cold at his intent gaze sweeping over her body from head to toe, lingering longer on her pants.

"For some strange reason, I believed I could make a woman out of you by taking away your britches. But I realize now the falsehood of my reasoning."

"So, are you saying you'll be leaving me to decide my own future, including choosing my own clothes?"

He frowned. "To some extent, yes. But I also realize you wearing a gown rather than men's britches won't make a bit of difference in changing your state of womanhood. You are woman enough, even wearing britches, for any man, and quite beautiful. Have you an adequate wardrobe of gowns?"

She nodded. She'd worn her mother's gowns whenever she and her father dined together. They were years old. Still, she couldn't see the sense of purchasing new ones when her mother's dresses were serviceable. She knew she'd inherited her father's practical side concerning money, but she also possessed her own 'less is better' mentality regarding possessions. The one place she never scrimped, however, was the necessary equipment for running the ranch.

"Good." He smiled. "It wouldn't do at all for you to wear britches during your courtship, now would it?"

"Perhaps, though most of the men in Bozeman know me and don't seem to care how I dress. I don't think it'll make a bit of difference. Excuse me. I've household chores to do."

"Of course you do." He rose from his chair.

"May I ride the range tomorrow? You see, my hands require my assistance in the mending of fences in several places on my property—before Fall arrives."

"We shall see what tomorrow brings," he replied.

CHAPTER 4

*M*att reluctantly allowed Laura to return to ranch work the
following day, on the condition she return home early to
prepare their supper. He was puzzled by the fact that she pushed herself to
perform men's work, yet she'd easily taken to cooking and cleaning. He
recalled how she'd already set the table and had prepared breakfast by the
time he came downstairs this morning. He'd expected her to be elated when
he told her she could return to her work outdoors, but that she shouldn't
tire herself out. That was why she had ranch hands, he'd added. It seemed to
take her an inordinate amount of time to make her way out the door this
morning.

He thought about the Woodbury family Bible he'd found in the library,
and Laura's brother. He'd been told by Laura's solicitor she had been
wearing britches since her brother's death, which spoke volumes. Matt
believed she was trying to be the boy her father had lost—why, he had no
idea. But he planned to find out. He just hadn't found a delicate way to
broach the topic.

Matt envisioned how meaningless his life would be without Jonathan
and felt sympathy for Laura. It seemed everyone she'd ever loved in life
had died.

By mid-afternoon, he'd returned to the ranch, hot and sweaty, in dire need of a long cold drink and a soothing bath. His brown suit and slacks and patterned waistcoat were dusty from the plains where he'd worked, supervising his crew of men. For a fleeting moment, the practicality of dressing in dungarees and a cotton shirt came to mind, but not for long. It had been drilled into him since he was a kid that clothes made the man, even though he sub-consciously rebelled at the idea.

Just as the house came into view, he was greeted by the sight of Laura and a fair-haired man. They sat side by side on her front porch, enjoying tall glasses of lemonade. Matt's mouth fell open at the sight of her. She wore a white dress, full-skirted and sprigged with yellow flowers. But what truly caught his attention was her hair, which she'd left hanging down over her shoulders. All he wanted to do was bury his fingers in the silken tresses. She was a beautiful woman. It wouldn't be long before the entire town of eligible men wanted to court her. He wondered why they hadn't pursued her before now.

Matt left the horse he'd ridden that day with one of the grooms and strode toward the house, eyes narrowed on the man sitting far too close to Laura.

Laura looked away from the man, laughter in her eyes. She sobered when she saw Matt. They rose to their feet, their gaze on him as he climbed the stairs.

"Mr. Black," Laura said, "I'd like you to meet Mr. Andrew Cravens. Andrew? This is my...my guardian, Matt Black."

Matt gave Laura a wry look before turning to shake the man's proffered hand. Sizing him up, Matt determined the man to be years older than his ward and himself.

Releasing Cravens' hand, Matt gave Laura a pointed look. "So, how long have the two of you known each other?"

"Actually, we're the best of friends and have known each other for years, haven't we, Andrew?"

Andrew nodded.

"Old family friends, are you?" Matt inquired.

"Yes. Andrew owns the ranch adjoining ours."

"I see," was all Matt could think to say, disgusted with himself, and his rising jealousy toward a man he didn't know. All he knew was that he didn't like him sitting so close to Laura.

Matt leaned against the railing.

Laura said, "Would you care to join us in a glass of lemonade?"

"Yes, I would. Thank you." Matt folded his arms, staring at Cravens. When Cravens met his gaze straight on without flinching, Matt had to admit to admiring the man. Upon closer inspection, Matt decided Cravens had an honest look about him, and that he could trust him with Laura.

"So, then," Matt said, breaking the silence, "how is the ranch business?"

Cravens smiled. "We grow the same crops and raise the same kind of steer as Laura does. I'm turning a profit, if that's what you're asking." At Matt's nod, he added, "My place isn't quite as profitable as Laura's, but then I didn't discover a sapphire mine on my property."

"I see." *So that's how Laura came by the name Princess Sapphire!* Matt made a note to himself to ask Laura about it.

By the time Laura returned, Cravens had left. She paused in the doorway and looked around with a frown. "You scared him off, didn't you?"

Matt took the glass of lemonade and sank into a chair. "No, he left of his own accord. He said to convey his apologies, but he had to leave for another engagement."

He took a deep, long swallow before setting the glass down on the railing. Then he reached inside his pocket and pulled out a neatly folded piece of paper. "Here's a list of eligible men I investigated shortly after I arrived."

She stared at him in disbelief. "You had them investigated?"

"Ah, yes, I see I approved your Mr. Cravens. Here is a list of tentatively approved candidates for a husband. You likely know some of them."

Laura set her own glass down, took the paper and unfolded it. She frowned at the first one, scowled at the next, laughed outright at the third. With a sigh, she met his gaze. "I'll agree to an outing with each of them, if that's what you want."

"It is," Matt said, narrowing his eyes on her. "I'm glad to see you can be agreeable."

"I believe my father always thought me quite amiable. I don't think you'll find that I'll give you too much trouble."

Matt cleared his throat. "You know, Miss Woodbury, you and I are closer in age than not. I'd like you to call me Matt."

She smiled. "I agree, and I'm Laura."

"It's amazing," Matt said good-naturedly. "We agree on something."

"Yes, amazing. Now tell me how you plan on 'weeding' out the gold-diggers from the men who are sincere."

"I have my ways. You'll see."

September 1886

Ｗith the arrival of autumn, the last hot days of summer had been left behind. And still Laura hadn't found a man worthy to be her husband. Matt's work for the railroad was nearly done and soon he'd be returning home to Minnesota. But he'd recently faced the truth of the matter. He didn't want to go home. This place, with Laura, was beginning to feel like home to him.

The four men on his potential list of suitors hadn't worked out. Would Paul Johnson, the man currently courting Laura—a wealthy widower with a ranch twice the size of the Woodbury Ranch—be the man for her?

As he'd done with each candidate, he started ticking off the good and the not-so-good traits. Ironically, both he and Laura had been in agreement as to the faults of each man. He knew the reason why. Matt was more than a little attracted to her and, venturing a guess, he had a feeling she was equally attracted to him. She was easy to be with—once she'd gotten over the shock of him being declared her guardian.

She was lovely, Matt thought, from where he sat on her front porch. Then he thought about his first love—his wife, Sarah. She'd been the only woman he'd ever loved, until six years ago when she'd left him and their sickly son behind, for a wealthy man. The boy was now a healthy, robust child of seven, and Matt missed him acutely.

After Sarah left him, he'd asked himself if he'd done something wrong to drive her away. He'd never arrived at an answer to his question, which perplexed him. He decided, in the end, that she'd fallen out of love with him and in love with another. He'd been devastated, for he'd loved her. He'd eventually concluded that what she really wanted was a wealthier life than he could ever give her. So he'd sworn off women, refusing to risk his heart again—until now.

There was much to admire about Laura. He appreciated her hard work ethic, her honesty with him and the workers on her ranch. She possessed an enchanting sense of humor and even laughed at her own blunders. On a daily basis, he found himself fighting his strong attraction and ever-growing feelings for her. Yet he knew that, sooner or later, he'd have to open his heart and take a chance on love again. He had no desire to live the rest of his life alone.

So what should he do? Coming to a decision, he nodded. He'd make an offer for her hand. While Laura hadn't been blatantly obvious, he knew she held equal admiration and respect for him. Whether it was his looks, his humor, his sense of duty and justice, he had no idea, but he guessed her feelings for him were based on all those things. But love? No, she probably didn't love him yet. Their attraction for each other would be enough for now. With time, he was convinced they'd fall in love, eventually.

He would assist Laura in managing the ranch and continue his work for the railroad but give up the lumber business, which was waning anyway. There was something about this untamed territory that drew him to it. He loved his home in Minnesota, but he had a feeling he'd experience much more of life staying in Montana. He'd send a wire tomorrow to his parents, instructing them to ready Jonathan for the journey to Montana. They'd been apart long enough.

A horse's pounding hooves caught his attention. He glanced sharply toward the road leading to the ranch. A lone horse galloped toward him. Seeing Laura was the rider, he rose from his chair and ambled down the steps to meet her. Eyeing the horse, he knew it wasn't hers.

"How was your supper with Mr. Johnson?" he asked.

"Fine," she said shortly, swinging down from the horse and meeting him at the foot of the steps.

Raising one eyebrow, he stared down at her. "Then why have you returned so early? It's just half past seven."

There was an unnatural flush to her cheeks. Reaching out, he took her hand and pulled her up the steps and into the house. From the grim look on her face, something was wrong.

In the foyer, he asked, "What happened?"

She swept her hair back from her forehead and tossed her reticule down on a small side table. "Paul Johnson is not the man for me, I'm afraid." She frowned. "Oh, the evening began well enough and, really, we have so much in common, I suppose, because we both own big ranches, but that's about all."

"Did he hurt you?" Matt said, keeping his voice calm when he wanted to shout. "Why didn't he escort you home?"

"This is his horse. He's drunk as a skunk and is currently head-first in a horse trough back in town. I can't marry a man who drinks like that, and in the afternoon of all things! It was only a luncheon we were having, and, he'd taken liberties, I am afraid."

"Damn him."

"Don't get yourself all dandered up. I took good care of him."

Matt could see now she was irritated but hadn't been harmed. He smiled. "Tell me what happened—over a libation would be helpful."

"I think I'd prefer lemonade, if you don't mind," she said wryly.

He escorted her into the library, then left, returning with a glass of lemonade for her and a sherry for himself. Sinking down beside her on the divan, he noticed the sad look on her face. His heart wrenched when she asked, "Why can't I find a decent man to love me, Matt? Am I so unlovable?"

"Of course you're not," he said gruffly, not quite sure how to respond. "Isn't it only because of me that you're looking for a husband anyway?"

Laura smiled. "It is, but not because of you precisely. I've lived my entire life trying to keep my father happy. And, now that I've allowed myself to be courted, I have to admit I enjoy it. I see now that I was spending too much time working and not having any fun." She scowled and added, "Though I wonder if things might have worked out between me and John if you hadn't scared him off."

Matt admitted, "All right, I may have been wrong in running him off as I did, but, according to your father's will, he expected you to marry a man of wealth and position. I don't believe a ranch foreman qualifies."

He thought about her lament about being unlovable. He wanted to tell her he wanted to be the one who'd love her forever—and maybe this time that would be true.

"Of course you were lonely after your father died. But I believe I have a solution," he said. "None of those men was right for you. I've a man in mind, though, one I believe who will be."

Laura's eyes widened. "Truly? Who?"

Matt gauged her expression and said staunchly, "Me."

CHAPTER 5

hough surprised, she didn't laugh because his offer wasn't funny. His suggestion was so unexpected she wasn't quite certain how to respond. Finally, she thought she understood why he'd made it. "Matt, you mustn't sacrifice yourself for me. I'll find someone worthy, as you say, sooner or later."

He scowled and leaned forward, bracing his elbows on his knees. "Sacrifice? What are you talking about? My marrying you is the answer to this dilemma."

She shook her head and heaved a sigh. "No, it would be a sacrifice, because of the duty you feel toward me and to your uncle."

He rose rigidly from his chair and said, "You're rejecting my offer?"

Laura bit her lower lip and nodded. She set down her glass on the table beside her, refusing to meet his eyes.

"Why?"

Tears flooded her eyes. *Because it is duty and not love you feel for me!* "Because I refuse to be the sort of woman you want. Wearing gowns and pretending to be a gentle woman satisfied with household duties. That's not my life. I'm not that sort of woman. Because you deserve to be married to a woman who *does* love you. Because we both deserve to be in love with the people we marry."

Holding her gaze with his, he said, "You could be that woman."

She shook her head and drew away. "No, I gave up that life years ago."

He straightened. "Because that was what you wanted?"

"I had no choice. My father needed me working beside him."

"Why? He had a foreman."

She rose from the divan. Crossing to a window, she looked out into the night. "The foreman always has been second in command—I've been first."

"I see. And where was your father during all of this?"

She faced him. "Managing the books and such."

Moving to her side, he took her hands in his. "But why? He was a healthy man, wasn't he? A hard-working man, I've been told. What caused him to lock himself away in his library all those years ago, leaving you the burden of operating the ranch?"

Laura choked back her tears. "He wasn't well." She pulled at her hands until he released them. "Stop questioning me. It's none of your business."

"But I want you for my wife. That makes it my business, especially since you've turned down my proposal. I deserve to hear the truth. Trust me with your secrets," he murmured, drawing her close once more.

If a heart could break, she knew hers would. Her body began to shake. And when she melted in his arms, he tightened his grip on her. She realized Cupid's arrow had struck her fast and hard. There wasn't a thing she could do about it. Much as she hadn't expected, nor desired to fall in love with anyone—most of all him—she had.

After she'd sobbed against his chest for some time, she pulled away from him and swiped at his lapels with a shaky hand. "Oh! I've wet your coat," she said in distress.

"Doesn't matter. Look at me."

She forced herself to meet his gaze.

Searching her face, he stroked her hair back from her forehead. Comfort flooded her at his tenderness. Then he shocked her out of her shoes by saying, "Tell me about Jeremy."

———

h God, who told him?

Laura closed her eyes and pressed her forehead against the center of his chest. "Let's go out on the porch. I need some air."

"Of course," he said, escorting her outside. She sank down in one of the wicker chairs. He sat on the railing, leaning against a post as he patiently waited for her to answer him.

She sighed, glad he chose to distance himself a bit from her. The telling of the story would be easier to tell. For once she felt confident that here was a man who could lift her burdens from her shoulders. A man she could trust. One she could love.

As though he sensed she had no idea how or where to begin, he spoke. "I found your family Bible in the library with the notes about Jeremy's birth and death. I also saw the pictures."

She nodded. "Of course you did. He was my brother—my twin, actually —my soul mate and best friend. I miss him still, even though he's been gone for six years."

"Gone for as long as your father had locked himself away, you mean?"

Laura nodded. "I suppose people could look at it that way. But you couldn't blame my father. You see, I'm the one responsible for Jeremy's death."

Matt raised his brow. "How?"

Haltingly, she began, "It happened the summer we turned thirteen. It was a scorching day, I remember, in mid-July. Jeremy had been working with my father and the hands all day, moving from one chore to the next. It was Jeremy's first taste of what it would be like to be in complete command of a ranch. At the end of the day, Jeremy returned before my father did and sat with me on the porch, complaining of the heat. I could see he was sweaty and exhausted—I'd felt the same even though I hadn't been working out in the heat of the day. He suggested we take a dip in the river, even though Father had forbidden us. The river ran a fast current, and I wasn't the best of swimmers. Jeremy, though, was superb.

"I told him we shouldn't. It was dangerous, and father had forbidden it. He ignored my misgivings and convinced me we'd do little more than just sit on the river bank and dunk our feet. Once we arrived, though, Jeremy jumped right into that oasis. I waded in after him, staying in the shallows, while Jeremy swam out deeper. I called to him to come back. I don't know whether he heard me or not, but he kept on going while I crept closer to the bank, afraid for him." She paused, tears filling her eyes. "Suddenly his head went under the water and never came back up. I couldn't see him anywhere. He was just…gone. We…we found him a week later, washed up onto a bank a few miles away." She swiped at her tears. "We figured an undertow had taken him."

Matt pulled her up from the chair to hold her loosely in his arms. "It was an accident."

"One I could have prevented if I had insisted we stay home," she said.

"Your brother chose to go. Do you think he would have stayed home if you'd tried keeping him there?"

Laura shook her head. "No. Still, I let my father down. For years he counted on me to watch over Jeremy." Dryly, she added, "I was always the sensible one—actually more of a mother to Jeremy than a sister—even though we were the same age."

"Still, I can't see how your father could blame you for the accident."

"He never actually said anything accusatory to me, but I saw that look in his eyes. Why wasn't it me and not his son? So, I remade my life, choosing to work alongside my father, until he lost interest in the ranch and shut himself away from everyone. Then I was forced to take charge of it, which wasn't a hardship. I love my home, Matt."

"You were trying to replace your brother."

She nodded, biting her lip. She'd spent years trying to be a good daughter—forsaking her own femininity to be the son taken from her father.

"None of this changes how I feel about you," Matt murmured.

Laura felt the squeeze of his hands at her waist and she managed a smile. "I guessed as much. You are a very persistent man, Mr. Black."

He grinned. "True, but it's always been a help rather than a hindrance."

Her smile disappeared. "Do you love me?"

Laura's heart plummeted at the annoyance and uncertainty that suddenly appeared on his face. He didn't love her, which would make things impossible between them. She'd never marry a man who was unsure of his feelings for her. He either loved her or he didn't.

He released her and turned away. She suppressed the urge to run inside. She knew he wasn't a gold-digger. Shortly after Matt's arrival, she'd spoken with her solicitor about Matt and learned he was a well-to-do man himself.

Matt paced from one end of the porch to the other, seemingly deep in thought. Laura bade her time, waiting for him to reply.

He halted then, hands clasped behind his back, and finally looked directly at her. "I believe I do love you."

"Oh, Matt!" Laura gasped, tears once again filling her eyes.

"Yet I must tell you I've had little success in love."

She frowned. "I don't understand."

"You see—" Matt began, pausing to look off toward the road.

Laura heard it then, the sound of wheels and horse hooves pounding the ground. A carriage appeared, made the bend in the road and headed toward the ranch. Beneath the horseshoe gateway, it came closer. The small cherub face of a child capped by curly blonde hair appeared at the window. A boy shouted, "Papa! Papa!"

Matt bounded off the porch and tore down the drive, meeting the coach. It stopped, and the door opened. Matt swept the child out of the carriage and into his arms. Laura saw the child was male, dressed in a fine blue suit and white shirt that was in dire need of a washing. He also wore a straw hat over his curls, banded in matching blue grosgrain.

Laura was stunned. Matt had a child? Why hadn't he told her before now?

Laura felt frozen in her position on the porch. She wrapped her arms around a post as she watched man and child embracing. A small smile slid across her lips when the boy pounded his father on the back in delight. Matt set the boy down, took his hand and walked toward the house. The boy was tall and older than she'd originally thought, appearing to be of early school age. He climbed the stairs on long, coltish legs with Matt directly behind him. They stopped before her.

"Laura, this is my son," he said with a gentle smile. "Jonathan, this is Miss Laura Woodbury."

"How do you do, ma'am?" Jonathan said. Stepping forward, he held out his hand.

Reaching down, she hesitantly took his hand in hers. "It's nice meeting you, too," she murmured.

They released hands simultaneously. Laura couldn't take her eyes from Jonathan, who was utterly handsome and charming, like his father. But where Matt's hair and coloring was dark, Jonathan was pale and blonde. Must take after his mother, she assumed. Speaking of the boy's mother, she sent a pleading look at Matt.

"I'm not married, if that's what you're thinking," he explained.

"Oh, I'm sorry," she whispered as she sat down. "I didn't know you were a widower."

"I'm not," he said, his gaze moving to his son, then back to her.

Curiosity settled deep inside her. She wanted to hear his story but knew now was not the time, with the boy in hearing distance.

Matt took the chair beside Laura while Jonathan sat on the wood floor.

Laura smiled when one of the new kittens sat down beside him. The boy laughed. Laura's smile widened when the kitten settled down on his lap.

"Jonathan will be seven on Christmas Day. The day he was born was, needless to say, the happiest Christmas for me," Matt said. "He's an easy child to love."

Yes, children—Jeremy. Oh, how she'd missed her brother after he died—still did. The pain had been deep, filling her with remorse at her loss.

The sound of horse's hooves pulled her from her reveries.

Amery Hawkins, one of her hands, stopped at the porch, tipped his hat to her and said, "The south pasture fence is fixed, Miss Laura."

"Good," she replied.

Jonathan stood up, still holding the cat, all his attention on Amery's horse. He glanced at his father. "May I ride a horse, Papa?"

"Another day, son."

Jonathan put down the kitten and walked down the steps toward the horse. Amery dismounted and said, "Okay if I take the boy with me while I rub down Swifty here?"

"Only if Jonathan promises to obey everything you tell him," Matt said.

"Oh yes, Papa! I will, I will!"

As Laura watched the excited boy walk off with Amery and the horse, it occurred to her that Jonathan had to have come here because Matt had sent for him. His arrival so soon after Matt had proposed now began to seem suspicious to her. She waited until Jonathan had moved away before blurting, "So, in all truth, you aren't really looking for a wife, Matt. You're really looking for a mother for your son."

Matt riveted a cold look on her, one she hoped she'd never see again. When he spoke, it was clear she'd made a mistake. "If that were the case, I'd have married years ago. It's you I want. If you look deep inside yourself, you'll see you want me, too. But I've asked, and I won't beg. Think about it. Think about us."

Matt turned from her, took the stairs in two steps and hurried after his son.

---

*T*ension permeated the parlor where Laura and Matt sat on opposite ends—he in one chair—she in her rocker. After she'd prepared a meal for them all, Matt had managed to lull an excited yet exhausted Jonathan to sleep within minutes. Now Matt sat reading the newspaper. She rocked in her chair and darned a pair of stockings she'd pulled from a bushel basket, burning to talk with him. He'd talked only to his son at supper, and since then he'd been silent, seemingly engrossed in his paper.

Laura was sorry she'd blurted out what she had, but it was hard to believe that hadn't crossed Matt's mind. She hadn't meant to upset him, but it did have to be discussed. Because, the truth was, she suspected she was falling in love with him. *Was* in love with him. It'd happened slowly, over the past three months, each time she compared him to one of her suitors. Simply put, there was no comparison.

"I heard some of your hands talking today," Matt said. He folded the newspaper and set it on the table at his elbow. "Why do they call you Princess Sapphire?"

Finally! No more silence. Laura dropped her darning in her lap. "My father discovered gold on our property shortly after he purchased it thirty years ago. Ten years later, in the same mine, he found sapphires—quite a treasure he learned, after sending samples to Tiffany's in New York City. My father hired a crew to work the mine. Men still travel here from afar to see if more of the gems can be found, though it's been dry for five years. It's one of the more difficult jobs our ranch hands perform—keeping the sapphire-seekers off our property. Everyone in these parts knows my father made a fortune from the sapphire discovery. Suddenly, our hands started calling me Princess Sapphire, in jest, but the name stuck. I know it's silly."

"I'd say it's accurate, Laura. You are a precious jewel, whether you realize it or not." He turned away and stared into the fire crackling in the hearth.

"Matt?"

He met her eyes again. She noted his hesitant expression, as though he knew what her next words would be. "What happened between you and your wife?"

"I divorced her when she left me for another man," he said.

Divorced? This was something Laura knew little about. People just didn't get divorces out here. Married folk stayed married until one of them died.

"Jonathan was born early, weighed less than four pounds. We didn't think he was going to make it, but he did." He grinned. "He's a fighter, same as me. Sarah was several years younger than I, much too young to be married to me, or anyone else for that matter.

Our parents were friends and the match was more or less arranged by them. I came to believe that Sarah was actually in love even then, when we married, with the man she later left me for. I didn't understand any of this at the time and, when I began to, it was too late. By then she'd grown tired of being married to a man she didn't love. Adding the burden of being a mother to a sick infant was too much for her. She left with this man, who just happened to be able to give her far more than I could. Anyway, I wasn't the man she wanted to be with."

"I'm sorry," Laura said sincerely as she picked up her darning once more.

"So am I. But it happened years ago. I forgave her, Laura. After all, our courtship and marriage was pre-arranged. And she did bless me with a son."

"Jonathan is wonderful," she said, smiling at the proud look on Matt's face.

He turned to her, sweeping his gaze over her face, and smiled in return. "You'd make Jonathan a wonderful mother, Laura."

Laura's body went icy at the thought. Inside, she heard herself scream, No! Never again would she allow herself to give into her maternal instincts. Everyone she'd ever cared for—Jeremy, her father, and even the mother she'd never known—were gone. She knew if she ever loved a child again and had the responsibility of caring for him, she wouldn't be able to bear the heartache if she lost him.

"Did you hear what I said?" Matt asked.

Laura dropped her darning in her basket and came swiftly to her feet. Snatching up her skirts, she headed toward the doorway, saying, "I can't talk about this, Matt. Not now." *Perhaps not ever.*

Matt scowled as he tossed down his paper and rose to his feet. "Have you even considered my proposal?"

She paused at the door, hand on the knob. "I have. I can't marry you, for one simple reason."

"Why?" he asked.

She heard the hurt and confusion in his voice and nearly blurted out the truth. Instead, she gathered herself to tell a lie. "I don't love you. I refuse to marry any man without love." She gave a raw laugh. "It would be a mistake."

"You don't know that," he said, striding toward her.

Laura held up her hand, palm up. "Stop, Matt, now, before I say something I'll regret—before I say something that will cause you to hate me forever."

He stopped directly in front of her. "I don't understand you. I don't think you understand yourself. But perhaps you're right that we shouldn't marry." He shrugged carelessly. "Perhaps you require more time to mature before taking that step. But I know you love me, Laura. From deep inside my soul, I know it. In two weeks, my work here will be done, and Jonathan and I will be leaving."

Frowning, she said, "Why did you have him travel all this way if your work was near completion?"

"Because, fool that I am, I assumed you'd accept my proposal. I know how much your ranch means to you and I guessed you wouldn't leave with me. There's a position with the railroad currently open right here in Bozeman. I was ready and willing to assist you in the running of the ranch as well." He sighed. "Everything would have been perfect. And now I'll be leaving, filled with guilt." His words held a bitter tinge.

"Why? What would you feel guilty about?"

"I'm leaving you without a husband. I've always fulfilled my duties in life, but I've failed this time. Paul can be no more disappointed in me than I am in myself."

"If it would help, I'll write to Mr. Hill and explain things to him." She blinked back tears, all the while wanting to cry out that she loved him, that she'd marry him and give him more children, but she couldn't. Her father had died, Jeremy, her mother. Everyone she'd ever loved had left her. She couldn't take another chance on loving again. And the responsibility of mothering another child left her feeling cold with fear.

"I appreciate all that you've tried to do for me, Matt. Never doubt that you performed your duty well."

Two weeks later

*a*t the train station in Bozeman, Jonathan sat beside Matt. He scuffed his feet forward, then dragged the toes of his boots back across the floor.

"Stop it now, Jonathan," Matt said, for the tenth time in as many minutes. "It won't make the train arrive any quicker."

"I wanna go back to Miss Laura's house, Papa. I miss her kitty."

Matt slid his arm around his son's shoulders. "I promise that, as soon as we arrive home, I'll find you a kitten. Or perhaps a dog would be better?"

"No, don't want no stupid dog and no other kitty." Tears flooded Jonathan's eyes, and he sobbed, "I want Miss Laura's kitty!"

Matt pulled the boy against his chest, feeling like crying himself. Not over a kitten, but over a woman. A fine woman who drove him mad with desire, mad with anger. Never had he met such a stubborn wench as

Princess Sapphire. And poor Jonathan had been whining off and on during their time together at Laura's ranch during the past couple weeks. Matt knew the reason. Jonathan had missed him during his three-month absence and wanted all his attention. Matt vowed never to leave him behind again.

Matt watched a procession of ants crawl across the cement floor, until a pair of black boots appeared in his line of vision. He looked up and into the dry expression on Andrew Craven's face.

"Cravens," Matt said by way of greeting. He glanced at Jonathan, who was settled against his shoulder, relieved to see he'd fallen asleep. He released him and eased him gently down on the bench seat, positioning his jacket beneath his son's head.

"So, you're just leaving her to fend for herself, are you?" Andrew said, his voice laced with sarcasm. "Didn't figure you for a quitter, Black."

Matt rose to his feet, coming toe to toe with the smaller man. "What did you call me?"

"You heard me the first time—quitter."

Matt couldn't get into a fight, not with Jonathan here. Calmly, Matt said, "Look, I'm leaving for home with my son. The territory's clear for you to pounce once more upon Miss Laura. It turns out she's pretty smart about people. Whether or not she gives you a second look is entirely up to her."

Andrew shrugged. "So, you didn't believe her when she said we were nothing but good friends."

"No, I didn't. You seemed too cozy at the time on that porch."

With a sigh, Andrew said, "I suppose she didn't happen to mention I'm engaged to her second cousin, Nadine, either, did she?"

Swiping an errant lock of hair off his forehead, Matt glowered at him. "You aren't lying about this, are you? Because if you are…"

"Nope, it's the truth. Now I hear the town talk—folks are saying you and her would be a good match. What do you think?"

"That might have been true once, but not anymore. She turned down my proposal."

"Go back to her. If you can't shake an honest answer out of her as to why, then talk to her maid, Mary O'Garrity. She knows everything."

"What's to tell? I told you I asked her to marry me and she declined."

"I know you've no reason to trust me but missing this train will be the best thing you could do. Go back and talk to her."

"Why do you care?" Matt said.

Andrew shrugged. "Guess I've got a protective streak in me with regards to Miss Laura. Sure wouldn't want her getting taken advantage by some gold-digger. You know?"

"Yeah," Matt said, a slow grin crossing his lips. "I do."

CHAPTER 6

*M*att returned with Jonathan to Laura's ranch. Now he sat in the parlor taking tea with Mary O'Garrity. Jonathan, of course, was in heaven as he sat on the floor with Laura's kitten once more. Damn, if Andrew Cravens was fooling with him, he'd personally go back and shoot the man. Even worse would be the hell he'd pay pulling Jonathan away from the ranch again.

"It's glad I am to see ye have returned, Master Black."

"Mister Black or even Matt is fine, Mrs. O'Garrity."

"In Ireland it would be Master, mind ye, but Matt it is."

Matt chuckled, catching the twinkle in the older woman's eyes.

"So, it seems ye haven't given up on Miss Laura after all. Good!"

"I had," Matt said candidly, "until I ran into Andrew Cravens at the train station. He encouraged me to come back and talk with you before making a final decision to leave or not. Said you'd know everything."

She sighed. "Yes, I do," she said softly. "Did ye ask Miss Laura to marry ye?"

"I did."

"And she turned ye down, didn't she?"

"Yes. Is she out with the hands now?"

"She is. The funny thing was, I had to drag her out of bed this morning.

44

Since ye came and introduced her to lady-like things—something I've tried doing fer years—she seems to have lost interest in running the ranch. She works too hard, ye know."

"I do know, yes, and I don't like it one bit," he growled. "Explain why you believe she turned down my marriage proposal. She told me she didn't love me."

Mary shrugged. "Now that, I'm telling ye, is a bald-faced lie. Miss Laura's in love with ye, for sure. Never have I seen her look at a man the way she looks at ye."

Matt felt heat seep into his cheeks at her words and had no idea how to reply.

"She's turned down every man who's ever proposed to her. I always attributed it to the fact that she's too fickle, but I've learned the truth of the matter directly from her, mind ye."

Leaning forward, his elbows on his knees, he stared at Mary. "What truth?"

"She blames herself fer Jeremy's death."

Frowning, Matt said, "I knew that. She told me about it."

"Jeremy was young when he died. Did ye notice Miss Laura was, perhaps, a bit more amenable to accepting yer proposal before Jonathan arrived? Before she knew ye had a child?"

Matt thought about how their conversation had progressed just after he'd proposed to Laura. While she hadn't come out and accepted his proposal, he'd felt she would have—if Jonathan hadn't arrived when he had.

All of sudden, everything was clear in his mind. He met Mrs. O'Garrity's gaze. "Her reasons have to do with Jonathan then. He's young—a child—even younger than Jeremy had been when he died." Rising from his chair, he took a step, then stopped. "I need to find Laura. Have you any idea where she's working?"

"Of course, the furthest pasture to the south of the river. Ye understand then. I'm glad. How will ye convince her?"

"I've no idea." He laughed. "Beg her probably. I just won't leave the ranch. She'll have to find someone big enough to boot me off the property."

"Now ye're talking, Master!" Mrs. O'Garrity said gleefully. "I'll keep an eye on Jonathan here."

"Thank you."

***

*L*aura slouched in the saddle upon her finest quarter horse, Charlie. A cool autumn breeze ruffled her hair, which she'd let down moments ago from its pins. She'd been pounding posts into dry ground for several hours. Now searing pain shot through her right arm and shoulder. It might be this particular injury would leave her unable to work alongside the men for a few days. Fine, she needed a rest, mostly to heal her injured heart more than her shoulder.

She sniffled and called out, "I'm leaving for the day, Pete!"

"You go right on home, Miss Laura. We'll be here just a few more hours."

"Thank you." she replied. Turning her horse around, she headed for home, comfortable that Pete was in charge.

For years, Peter Jorgenson had worked as third-in-command for her father and now easily assumed foreman responsibilities. To her, it seemed natural for him to assume the position. She hadn't thought of mentioning this to Matt earlier. There seemed to be so many things she hadn't thought of where Matt was concerned.

She ambled along the river bank, Charlie picking his way carefully along the uneven ground. Soon it would be time to cross the river, which she dreaded. Each time she had to cross, she thought about Jeremy, even though the river had little current in the area where she forded it.

Finally, she reached the small, narrow path leading down to the river bank. As she guided Charlie down it, he pranced and tossed his head. She heard another horse's hooves and looked across to the other side where a horse and rider came into view.

Matt!

Her heart ached and raced simultaneously at the welcome sight of his handsome face, with that brilliant, even-toothed smile she'd never forget. She called out, "What are you doing here?"

He didn't respond, likely because he hadn't heard her with the distance between them.

She stayed riveted in place, watching him as he approached, taking in his broad shoulders, and deep chest covered by his dark suit.

"Are you coming over here?" he called. "If you aren't, then I'm crossing to you."

Gathering her wits, she said, "Yes, I'm coming! Tell me why you've returned."

He paused, slouched in the saddle, one hand resting on the pommel. "To marry you, Princess Sapphire. You don't have to worry though. I'm no gold-digger."

Hadn't the man listened to her? Hadn't he paid attention when she told him in no uncertain terms she didn't love him? Apparently, he hadn't believed her. Oh, how she wanted to marry him. But, like the river between them now, her fears must keep them separated. How could she possibly be responsible for a child when... Her gaze dipped to the water in front of her, anxiety sliding along her nerves.

She stared down into the rippling river, remembering that fateful day six years ago. Remembering how, after Jeremy had disappeared beneath the water, she'd slumped down on the bank, rocking herself, screaming and sobbing her heart out.

Could she be responsible for a child now that she'd grown up? Did she want that responsibility? If she didn't say yes, she'd deny living life and being happy because of her fear of something that had happened when she was a child herself. If she didn't grasp for that happiness now, she knew it would never come her way again. There would never be another Matt.

"Did you hear me, Laura? You know I don't want your money."

"Yes, I know," she called back. "I'm coming over now."

Matt nodded, watching her as she made her way south a bit more, where she knew it was shallow with little current. Laura clicked her tongue, encouraging Charlie to step into the water. Glancing up, she saw movement behind Matt, realizing it was another rider on a horse. As they drew nearer, she gasped at the sight of Jonathan on her old dappled gray pony, Wylie.

"Papa! Papa!" Jonathan called out gleefully. Wylie was at a full out gallop, headed toward his father. "Look at me! I'm riding."

Matt's head whipped around, and he shouted, "Stop, Jonathan! Don't come any nearer. The bank is slippery."

The boy paid no attention, and the pony pounded to the left past Matt, skidding down the river bank, before Matt could grab the animal. The horse's neighing filled the air, along with Jonathan's shriek.

Laura felt as though she'd been hurtled eight years back in time as she watched Wylie slide down the bank sideways, dumping Jonathan, who rolled into the river where he began frantically splashing about, the current carrying him to the middle.

"Don't thrash, son!" Matt, off his mount, called out as he sloshed through the water. "Swim! You know how."

All Laura could think was that she couldn't allow either of them to die. The river water was cold this time of year. They had to get Jonathan out of there—fast. The pony had scrambled to his feet, seeming to stare at the floundering boy. Then she noticed the reins floating in the water. Jonathan must still be holding onto them.

"Wait, Matt! Jonathan's got hold of the reins yet. And Wylie, thank God, hasn't budged. Go on over to Wylie and—"

Matt shouted, "Jonathan! Do not let go of the pony's reins. Understand?"

Laura thought she heard the boy agree, but she wasn't sure. She moved along the bank and guided Charlie into the river, halting him as she neared Jonathan, knowing the river was too deep for the horse to make it any closer, she paused. "You'll be fine, Jonathan," she called to him. "Your father will get you out but keep hold of the reins."

She saw the boy was crying, and her heart lurched. Did he still have hold of the pony's reins? Luckily, Jonathan had fetched up on a sand bar.

She watched Matt guide Wylie up the river bank, while he pulled on the reins with his free hand. She sighed in relief when she saw Jonathan come off the sand bar, drawn by his father. The boy held on. Hand over hand, Matt pulled his son in.

What was she doing here when she could be helping? Laura guided Charlie from the water and cantered to her usual shallow crossing place. Once on the other side, near Matt, who was still hauling the boy in by the reins, she slid down the bank, waded in and grabbed Jonathan. The cold water had rendered him unable to stand, so she tugged him from the river. Matt swept him up into his arms.

Matt held him close, saying, "Now do you understand the rule about never riding by yourself? Whatever possessed you to follow me? And does Mrs. O'Garrity know you left the house?"

Jonathan shook his head. "She fell asleep, and I snuck out. I'm sorry. I won't ever do it again, Papa."

"Let's get you home," Matt said.

***

*D*ark shrouded the ranch house by the time they'd managed to relieve Jonathan's chills by placing him in a warm bath. He grew more animated and talked about his adventurous day in an excited voice. "I wasn't scared," he boasted. "Papa was there and so were you, Miss Woodbury, so I couldn't drown."

Once Jonathan was in bed asleep and the two of them heading for the parlor, Laura started feeling ill at the thought of Matt and Jonathan leaving on the noon train tomorrow. She was sure of her love for Matt, yet uncertain about taking on the responsibility of being a mother to Jonathan. Though she should have shared her doubtful feelings with Matt when he'd first proposed to her, it still wasn't too late. She'd been given a second chance to talk things through with him. This time she wouldn't run like a coward.

She sat on the divan and he joined her, one arm stretched out along the back, his fingers toying with a curl that had come loose from her chignon.

Laura felt his warm gaze on her. She turned to him and lifted her lips to his. Accepting the invitation, Matt kissed her thoroughly, gathering her into his arms. She breathed a relieved sigh, feeling loved and protected, as warmth coursed through her. If only the kiss could last forever! Raising one arm, she wound it around his neck, pressing her breasts against him. His hand wandered up her arm, brushed against the side of one breast until his hand cupped it. He rubbed her nipple with his thumb until she gasped her pleasure.

All too soon he let her go, springing to his feet to pace the floor. His fingers tunneled through his thick hair. Feeling deserted, not knowing why he'd left her so abruptly, she bit her lower lip, watching him, wondering what was wrong.

Finally, he stopped in front of her and said, "I won't take no for an answer—not this time."

She sighed in relief.

He sank down beside her once more. "Why did you turn me down?"

"I owe you an explanation. Perhaps it won't make a bit of sense to you, but it does to me. Remember when I told you I was responsible for my brother's death?"

"Yes, but it's not true."

"For years, I believed it was true. Even now…" She stopped. Maybe she'd feel that way forever, but guilt wouldn't bring back Jeremy. Now was for living. She slipped her hand into his and wound their fingers together. "I love you very much, Matt. When you asked me to marry you, I was so excited. I couldn't believe such happiness could be mine."

"Or mine," he murmured.

"Yet I doubted myself, doubted I could count on myself to be careful, conscientious and responsible for your son. I didn't want the responsibility on my shoulders for fear of losing him."

"The same way you lost your brother."

Laura nodded even as tears slid from her eyes and down her cheeks. After swiping at them, she met his gentle gaze. "Today, when Jonathan landed in the river, I felt like I was living that terrible moment in time all over again. I asked God above how could He be so cruel."

Pressing her to his chest, he murmured in her hair, "That's just it—you *did* come to help, and everything turned out all right. You are everything wise, wonderful and worthy, Laura Woodbury. Don't ever doubt your capabilities. There was no way you could have saved your brother, but you did help me save my son. Look how you've operated this ranch for the past several years. Look how profitable it's become. Look how your ranch hands respect you and your authority. Don't ever doubt yourself again. I won't allow it. And I'm convinced you'll be the best mother to my son, and to any children we will have. Believe in what I say, Princess. Believe in *yourself*."

"I'll try."

"Marry me, my sweet, precious jewel. Now is our time to be together."

She worried her lip a moment before asking, "What if I said I needed more time?"

He smiled. "I'd say that's a better reply than 'no.'" His smile slipped. "*Do you require more time?*"

Laura pressed her palms against his chest. "I was just teasing. I believe we've wasted too much time as it is. Yes, I'll spend the rest of my life with you, Matt Black, loving you, worrying about you and our children."

"Obeying me?" he asked, lifting one eyebrow.

"Perhaps," she said coyly.

"Ah, just what I expected. Stubborn to the end, but I wouldn't have you any other way, Princess Sapphire." His lips took hers. Laura's world narrowed, her heart, love and feelings all for this man.

They sat together on the divan, his arms around her as they enjoyed the silence, and the closeness between them. Laura would always feel responsible for Jeremy's death, but somehow, she now believed, Jeremy was watching them. She imagined seeing his brilliant smile, saluting her, telling her to get on with her life. To be happy.

Matt kissed her again, and she knew his love for her would sustain her for a lifetime. Nothing else mattered.

THE END

THANK YOU FOR READING

Did you enjoy this book?

We invite you to leave a review at the site from which this book was purchased.

DID YOU KNOW THAT LEAVING A REVIEW...

- Helps other readers find books they may enjoy.
- Gives you a chance to let your voice be heard.
- Gives authors recognition for their hard work.
- Doesn't have to be long. A sentence or two about why you liked the book will do.

Don't miss out on your next favorite book!

Join the Satin Romance mailing list

Subscriber Perks Include:

- First peeks at upcoming releases.
- Exclusive giveaways.
- News of book sales and freebies right in your inbox.
- And more!

Don't miss
The MacAulay Bride

In 1888, widowed Brianna MacAulay is an independent woman struggling to support her two sons. She turns her home into a boarding house, believing this will preserve her from accepting another unhappy marriage proposal. But her late husband's brother, Harrison MacAulay, has lusted after Brianna for years.

Now that his brother is dead, Harrison is determined to win and wed her. He journeys from Scotland to America to coerce her to move to his home in Edinburgh. She soon learns her sons are under his guardianship, a stipulation in her husband's will, and she has no choice but to move to Scotland.

Sexual sparks fly as their mutual attraction deepens, but just when Brianna is beginning to trust him, Harrison makes a critical mistake. Brianna tries to escape but Harrison holds her captive. He soon learns that love, not dominance, will win her heart.

Available where ebooks are sold.

Prologue

June 1, 1888
Winterhaven Manor, Edinburgh, Scotland

"My God, Raleigh," Harrison MacAulay said, "I feel as though I've just awakened from a bad dream, and none of what you have told me is true. Och! You are saying I must produce an heir or lose my home?"

"That's precisely what I'm saying," his solicitor replied. "It's right here, in your father's will, which he drafted when he was healthy and of sound mind, in case you have doubts."

Raleigh McKenna smoothed the parchment on the desk and read the old laird's words aloud. "My elder son, Harrison James McKenna, shall produce an heir by his thirty-first birthday. Otherwise, the MacAulay estates, including the ancestral home, Winterhaven Manor, shall accede to my second son, Payton Edward."

Harrison paced the green and gold Aubusson carpet, from one end of the walnut-paneled library to the other, a scowl firmly planted on his face. After a while, he paused and leveled his gaze on Raleigh. "Must I abide by this?"

Raleigh folded his hands on the desk and leaned forward. "If you expect to keep possession of your home and wealth."

"What in the world was the old man thinking, other than the fact he held a deep obsession at the prospect of becoming a grandfather?" Harrison raged. "Did you know Payton had contacted Father from America years ago and told him about his own two sons? Payton wrote to me and said he never received an acknowledgement from Father."

"You're not surprised by the lack of response from your father, are you? Your brother fought a duel, killed a man and left the country, never to be seen again. Not to mention leaving the family name tarnished."

"Not surprised at all. I was the one who took the brunt of my father's fury with Payton's leaving." Harrison would never forget that fateful day ten years ago. Payton had killed the husband of his latest mistress. In order to avoid repercussions from the law, and to save his own life, he was forced to flee Scotland.

"You do earn a decent living from your work as a physician. Would it be devastating to give up the home and lands to your brother?"

Harrison shrugged. "Not at all. I spend more time at my townhouse in Edinburgh than at Winterhaven, anyway, since my clinic is nearby. But have you any doubt that Payton would run the place into the ground?"

"I see your point." Raleigh grimaced. "That younger brother of yours has been undeniably irresponsible at times."

Harrison snorted in disgust. "And what about all the cousins who reside here? I took on the responsibility of supporting and raising the young ones when their families couldn't, not to mention my duty caring for our tenant families. Payton wasn't raised for the job. So, it appears I must marry, hmm?"

A frown creased Raleigh's forehead as he perused the document. "Don't see marriage mentioned at all."

That gave Harrison pause. "But would my heir be legal if I weren't married?"

"Of course! This is Scotland, man, not England!" Harrison's lips twitched at the irritable look on his solicitor's face as he continued, Hell, you could run off in an instant to Gretna Green and handfast, instead, for the required year and a day, then end the relationship."

Harrison scoffed, "Handfasting is an old tradition, but hardly legal."

"Yes, 'tis legal. Scotland's laws still recognize the tradition."

"If my handfasted wife provided me with an heir, would I be obligated to remain with her—to marry her officially after the fact?"

"No, not at all, which is likely why so many men have encouraged their lovers over the years to handfast instead of marry, I would imagine. Have you anyone particular in mind?"

"Perhaps."

"Connie MacPhearson?" he suggested.

Harrison heard the stiff tone in Raleigh's voice as he sank into a chair across from his friend. "Not even remotely."

Raleigh growled, "Och, are ye saying she's not good enough for ye?"

"Hell, no, certainly not," Harrison said, laughter in his voice. "Watch it, Englishman. You're starting to sound like a Scot. She would not have me because she's in love with you."

Sputtering, Raleigh jumped from his chair. "Now, see here... that is preposterous!"

"A moment ago you were ready to blow my head off at my response," Harrison drawled. "Thank God you hadn't a gun in your hand. When are you going to admit you're in love with the woman? You must know she's in love with you. The two of you are too stubborn for your own good, do you know that?"

"Enough," Raleigh snapped. "As your solicitor, I advise you to find a woman. Quickly. In eighteen months, you will be thirty-one. I'm leaving now. Do you require anything else?"

"No." Harrison rose and followed Raleigh to the door. "My thanks," he said, shaking his friend's hand. "I'll be making my decision soon."

After Raleigh left, Harrison stared out a long, narrow window, his hands folded behind his back. He watched his solicitor and long-time friend mount his horse and gallop away, all the while contemplating his choice of available womanhood.

Other than one particular woman who was always on his mind, none was appropriate. Brianna MacAulay was the only woman he'd thought about on a daily basis for the past ten years. The only woman he'd ever truly wanted yet had never met her—from the moment he'd seen her in the wedding picture Payton had sent to him.

It was truly unfortunate she was his brother's wife.

Chapter One

November 1888
Stillwater, Minnesota

Brianna MacAulay stood inside the train depot for the third afternoon in a row, watching passengers disembark from the last train of the day. She peered at the people swarming through the doorway, worried that some mishap might have befallen her husband's brother since she found no sign of the man.

There was nothing she could do now but go home and hope he would arrive tomorrow. She presumed it would then be a simple matter for him to settle her late husband's will. She frowned as she thought about the money she hadn't been allowed to withdraw from Payton's bank account. It was hers! She needed that money—every single penny—in order to furnish two more bedchambers in her home by spring. More lumberjacks would be arriving to work for the town's sawmills by then, and they would be in need of a place to stay.

Squaring her shoulders and hitching up her black taffeta skirt and petticoats, she walked toward the door and opened it. Huge drops of cold autumn rain splashed against her face and she squinted against the onslaught. For the little good it did, she held the umbrella over her head, bracing herself against the wind and rain. She sighed, wishing it were snow instead of rain. Snow wouldn't ruin the hat she wore. It was her favorite, with a bird's nest perched on top, its cloth occupant having long since flown away.

She dodged puddles on the deserted boardwalk before gingerly stepping into the muddy street, then rushed to her wagon. Upon reaching it, she held the umbrella in one hand as she placed a foot upon the running board, ready to board, when she heard a deep masculine voice shouting.

"Madam! A moment, please."

A big man wearing a top hat approached her. She lowered her foot and the umbrella just as he arrived at her side. He swept his cloak off his shoulders, held an edge of it high above her head, gallantly shielding her from the rain.

"I must speak with you," he said in a deep, accented voice.

As she peered up at him, she thought him familiar, but could not place him.

He took her elbow and nodded at Francis Marshall's Dry Goods. "Let us find protection."

Before she could dig in her heels, he fairly propelled her across the street, where they ducked beneath Marshall's dark green and white striped awning. Lord knew she should never have gone willingly with this stranger, yet she could not help but wonder why he had approached her. She tilted her head back to meet his eyes, but discovered them concealed behind a pair of rain-spattered, wire-rimmed spectacles.

Then he removed his hat and she recognized him—Harrison MacAulay, her brother-in-law. She'd never seen a picture of him, but the pleasant curve of his lips was very similar to her husband's, yet, with his smile the similarity ended. Where Payton had been fair-haired, blue-eyed and fine of build, Harrison was tall and broad-shouldered, his complexion darker.

Brianna's cheeks grew warm under his intent look and she gasped, "*You are Harrison MacAulay?*" From the moment he spoke, she should have guessed his identity because of his Scottish dialect.

"I am, dear sister-in-law," he said, inclining his head, "and at your beck and call for as long as you need me." He lifted her hand and brushed it with a gentle kiss.

She shivered. Her heart raced at his warm touch that she felt through the thin fabric of her glove. She pulled her hand away, not at all happy about the way his kiss caused a funny feeling inside of her. Of course, many women would have difficulty ignoring a handsome man of such extraordinary height, lean yet powerful build, black, wavy hair and deep brown eyes.

"I... I worried that something had happened to you." A sudden bolt of lightning splitting the sky startled her, and she added, "I suggest we leave for home before the roads become impassable."

He looked around, then met her eyes with a frown. "And where are your sons?"

"My neighbor, Mrs. Crane, offered to stay with them on the condition I return shortly."

"I apologize for my lateness. Two days ago, I boarded a train in Chicago. That was shortly after I sent the wire notifying you of my arrival. Alas, the train derailed and I was forced to wait for another that did not leave until this morning. I sent you a second wire."

"I never received it."

For some reason, she trusted his word, though she had long ago given up believing a single word from her husband. Payton had been a gambler and tippler, until he drowned a month ago in the St. Croix River. During the last two years of their marriage, she had learned to depend upon herself for her livelihood. Which was fine with her. She'd never been the sort of woman to sit idle day after day. Running the boarding house gave her something worthwhile to do, and she earned a fair living besides. The money she'd saved from her boarders was dwindling, though, and the next season's lumberjacks wouldn't be arriving for four long months.

"I suppose it could not be helped. Now, we must get out of this rain, although it doesn't matter since we are both thoroughly drenched."

He replaced his hat, took her arm and escorted her to her wagon, which luckily had a bonnet of sorts over the seats. "I must fetch my bags," he said, assisting her into the driver's seat. Within moments, he returned with two leather bags and tossed them into the back of the wagon. "Have you any suggestions regarding accommodations in town?"

"I wouldn't hear of you staying at a hotel. I've a room at home ready for you."

He raised his brow. "For propriety's sake, that may not be a good idea."

"My friends and neighbors wouldn't think poorly of me for offering a family member a place to stay." She saw the hesitant look on his face and she flushed, chiding herself for being so forward. She wanted him to stay with her, yet he appeared ready to decline. If he did, it would greatly disappoint her sons. They missed a man's presence in their young lives. As much as she hated to admit it, as much as she enjoyed her freedom, she missed a man in the house.

"Verra well. Then I shall see you later," he said and whacked Winney's hindquarters.

Brianna held onto the reins as the horse started moving forward and she shouted over her shoulder, "Aren't you coming?"

"I have business to tend to first."

"But you have no idea where I live!"

In the dimming light, she caught a flash of white and bristled when she realized he was smiling. "I'm certain I will have no trouble finding you."

As she headed for home, she couldn't help but wonder what business a stranger from Scotland could have in town with the approach of evening. From past experience where her husband was concerned, there were only a few reasons why a man went to town after dark. She shook her head and heaved a sigh, chagrined at her wayward thoughts. "All right, Brianna MacAulay," she muttered. "That will be enough of that sort of thinking."

~ * ~

Brianna stood in her parlor, satisfied that the cherry wood tables still glowed from her most recent polishing. The white lace curtains covering the windows were fresh and clean. The red, green and gold floral carpeting held nary a speck of lint. Her boys had their noses jammed against the parlor window as they anxiously awaited the arrival of their uncle.

"You will smear the glass, and after I just cleaned it," she scolded. "Now, come back to the kitchen and finish your supper."

"Not hungry, Ma," said seven-year-old Jamie.

"Me neither," announced Harry. The nine year old stared at her over his shoulder. "When did Uncle Harrison say he'd be here?"

She sighed and tried to count how many times they'd asked that same question since she arrived home more than an hour ago. "He didn't say. There will be no dessert if you don't eat the rest of your stew."

The boys turned to her, disappointment stamped on their faces. She crossed her arms and waited, fighting the urge to give into them. Admittedly, she indulged her boys—even understood her reasons for doing so. With the loss of their father, they seemed so sad much of the time, Harry, in particular.

Harry asked, "What's for dessert?"

"Do you not recognize the scent?"

Jamie inhaled and grinned. "Apple pie!"

She headed down the hallway, slowing at the sound of someone knocking on her door. She retraced her steps, but by the time she arrived at the door her sons had already opened it. They surveyed their uncle, small faces filled with suspicion, awe and curiosity.

Harrison's cloak hung over one arm. His black jacket fit his wide shoulders to perfection. A matching waistcoat, white shirt with crisp starched collar and gray tie completed his attire. He looked handsome, authoritative and wealthy.

Her younger son stuck out his hand. "I'm Jamie."

Brianna noted the pleased but melancholic expression crossing Harrison's face when he replied, "Jamie," and took his nephew's hand in his own. "You look remarkably like your father."

Brianna saw tears glistening in his eyes and thought how dreadful he must feel at the loss of his only brother he hadn't seen in ten years. She smiled when he reached down and swept Jamie into his arms, held him close. He closed his eyes and took a deep breath. He appeared to be inhaling the essence of her son's innocence, as one would inhale the sweet scent of a newly opened rose. Jamie allowed the affectionate embrace until Harrison lowered him to the floor.

She frowned when Jamie clung to his leg. "Your uncle cannot walk with you attached to him."

"He is fine where he is." He settled his big hand on Jamie's blonde thatch of hair, then turned to Harry, who stood by in silence.

"Greet your uncle, Harry," Brianna gently ordered.

"You don't look much like Pa," Harry blurted out, tilting his head to the side. "Except for your smile."

"Verra astute, my boy. I favor your grandfather, while your father took after your grandmother."

"I must also look like grandfather since I look like you."

From the moment Brianna had met Harrison at the train depot, she'd realized her eldest son's strong resemblance to his uncle. Until now, she'd always thought Harry resembled her.

Harrison opened his arms to welcome him, but Harry reached out, grabbed his hand and shook it, instead. Brianna saw fleeting disappointment cross Harrison's face before veiling it. "You know that your father named you after me, don't you?"

Harry shook his head. "Nope. I didn't." He grinned. "We were just going to the kitchen for dessert. Want some?"

"Depends on what it is."

"Oh, well, does it matter?" Harry asked, looking his uncle over carefully. "You look like you eat everything."

"Harry!" Brianna exclaimed, shocked.

Harrison threw back his head and laughed.

Harry's wide-eyed gaze never left his uncle. "But, Ma, he's big as old Farmer Jorgenson's ox!"

Brianna sighed, gave Harrison an apologetic smile. "Have you eaten supper yet?"

"Haven't had a bite since noon."

"How does beef stew, apple pie and coffee sound?"

He nodded. "Wonderful."

After the boys ate their pie and Harrison had finished his meal, the conversation was lively, interspersed with bouts of boisterous shouts and laughter. Brianna hated ending the evening. It had been a while since she'd seen her sons so happy. She hated doing it but at ten o'clock, she announced, "It's past bedtime, boys."

"Oh, but Ma, we don't have school tomorrow, and we want to talk more with Uncle!" Jamie protested.

"It is late," Harrison inserted. "I'll still be here come morning."

Brianna settled them down for the night and quietly made her way to her bedchamber. With a critical look, she examined herself in the oval mirror positioned over the cherry wood bureau, tucking a stray lock of black hair into the bun atop her head. While her sapphire-colored eyes were pretty and her short, straight nose was rather ordinary, she thought her high, wide cheekbones attractive. Enough, Brianna MacAulay! Whom are you trying to impress, anyway? Still, she pinched her cheeks before joining Harrison in the parlor.

He sat in a gold velvet gentleman's chair, which happened to be large enough to accommodate his bulk, one leg crossed over his knee, arms draped over the chair's arms. He rose upon her entrance and she took a seat on the threadbare crimson divan. He sat down again then. Brianna welcomed the heat from the fire he had stoked. Just the thought of kicking off her shoes and tucking her toes beneath her warm woolen blanket prompted her to close her weary eyes.

"Tell me about my brother. What caused his death?"

"If I could have kept him here with me he would not have died," she said, opening her eyes. "You received my letter, didn't you?"

"Aye, but you offered no explanation as to how Payton drowned, which I couldn't understand at all since he'd been an excellent swimmer."

"Drunk on spirits was the mortician's findings. He had difficulty controlling himself in that way."

"You mentioned if you could have kept him here with you, he wouldn't be dead. What did you mean?"

"He lived..." She hung her head, too embarrassed to continue.

"Go on," he prompted. Behind the spectacles, his eyes were kind.

"Your brother kept a mistress for the past two years. He spent little time at home."

"Ah, now why doesn't that surprise me?" he said dryly.

She raised her brow. "Are you telling me he had a history of womanizing?"

"Aye. But it is not all that uncommon in Scotland for a man to keep a mistress—discreetly, of course. This doesn't mean he doesn't love his wife. It's just that a wife is a lady, and a lady cannot always provide her husband... well... with what he needs."

The man was dreadfully serious. My Lord, he hadn't lived through the pain and agony of losing a loved one as she had. Not Payton's dying, but his leaving her for another woman. "Is that a fact?" she murmured. "May I assume a wife has the same privilege?"

He stared at her a long moment, confusion on his face, before asking, "What privilege would that be?"

"Why, to have affairs."

"Hardly," he snapped, rising to his feet.

She watched him pace the floor, tears filling her eyes even as her voice quivered. "I gave your brother my unequivocal devotion. I kept his home tidy and served him fine meals—that is, when he chose to bless us with his presence. But even that wasn't enough for him."

He paused in his pacing and stared at her. "How long have you been shouldering the burden for your family, Brianna?"

"For quite some time." She swallowed the lump in her throat and swiped at a tear running down her cheek. "Your brother had grand dreams of forging a fortune, and was well on his way to fulfilling them when he purchased stock in Mayor's Lumber Company. He grew fascinated with the every-day workings of that enterprise. In fact, he spent entire winters up north in the logging camps, working as a lumberjack. He loved being outdoors. But it meant him being away from home for so long. We all missed him terribly during those months, but he was working the work he loved. How could I deny him?"

Harrison frowned. "Payton didn't establish a solicitor's practice when he arrived in America?"

She raised her brow. "Payton was a lawyer?"

"Yes, a very successful one in Scotland, until he was forced to... until he decided to move to America. I had thought he'd start up his business here."

Payton had been educated? While his manners were exceptional, he always possessed a physically hard working man body. He'd never mentioned a word to her. Just thinking about his pay as a logger compared with what an attorney earned caused her to seethe.

Harrison encouraged her, "Continue, please."

"He would come home in the spring, as all the lumberjacks did, and stay until October when he'd leave again."

Harrison shoved back the edges of his jacket and jammed his hands deep into his pockets. "Are ye telling me that my brother left ye alone for more than half a year at a time?"

Ah, there was that burr again. She nodded.

"However did you manage?"

She lifted her chin and met his gaze straight on. "With difficulty."

After Payton's death, she had approached his solicitor, Reginald Nielsen. He'd told her everything had been taken care of, and that she need not worry her pretty little head about a thing. He'd also explained that until Harrison MacAulay arrived he couldn't release so much as a single cent to her.

"We shall call upon my solicitor first thing Monday morning," she announced, thinking of the money she required to purchase bed frames and mattresses from Sears Roebuck. A monthly charge of seven dollars per month, including board, was reasonable rent for a lumberjack. And renting five bedchambers would give her all the money she required to keep her home, and to feed and clothe her children.

"That will not be necessary since Mr. Nielsen and I have met, this very evening, in fact. We've straightened out Payton's financial affairs, and everything is in order."

Brianna frowned. "But Mr. Nielsen never conducts business past five o'clock, and never on Saturday or Sunday."

Harrison inclined his head. "He was willing to oblige me."

She clapped her hands in delight. "Well, that's wonderful news! Now you may return home to Scotland, and I may get on with my life."

He sat down beside her and gave her a gentle smile. "You seem to be an intelligent woman, and so I believe you will understand me when I say your financial situation is far from good." He reached inside his pocket and withdrew a small packet of money. "This is all that is left of Payton's estate, once Nielson paid off his considerable debts." He pressed the bills into her hand. "I'm sorry, but it will be necessary to sell your home. I've requested Mr. Nielsen to immediately begin seeking a buyer."

Staring in wide-eyed dismay at the paltry sum, Brianna rose from the divan. Clenching the money in her fist, she felt a fury unlike any she'd ever felt before threaten to ignite. "How could Payton do this to us?"

She thought how she'd tolerated her husband's drinking and gambling for the sake of their children, and because she loved him. In hindsight, she realized she had known little of love when she married Payton at sixteen. Recognizing her own shortcomings, she knew she was not as easy on the eyes as many other women. She had long ago come to terms with the fact that she would never be petite and pretty. Still, Payton's taking a mistress had hurt her. But then she also knew that she had been much more in love with Payton than he'd been with her. To this day, she still wondered why he'd requested her hand in marriage.

Sadly, the next time she saw him was after he'd drowned. She'd had him laid out in his blue serge suit, in a simple pine box. With tears rolling down her cheeks and her grieving sons on either side of her, she cursed him for having caused them all so much pain while he lived.

"I apologize for my brother's lack of responsibility for you and your sons. Payton never did possess one iota of common sense." He stared into the fire a moment before turning to her again. "A few years ago Payton sent me a letter regarding your welfare, if something were to happen to him. His desire was for you to return with me to Scotland."

"I am capable of taking care of myself and my sons. For two years I've taken in boarders and have done just fine, thank you." She swept past him and took and took up a place opposite him, on a straight-backed chair, folding her hands in her lap. She had to keep her distance from him. He attracted her... too much.

"You mean to tell me you open your home to strangers?" he asked, rising to his feet once more and headed toward her.

"I was forced to do so," she said, lifting her chin, meeting the fiery look in his eyes head-on. "This is my home and I'm not leaving it."

"Hell and damnation!" he growled, stopping directly in front of her. "Do you think I want to do this to you?" He raked a hand through his hair. "I hate uprooting you and your sons, but we have no choice in the matter. You've been left penniless, left with nothing but your children and, I'm afraid even they aren't legally yours.

"We leave for Scotland as soon as I can make arrangements," he stated firmly.

Want to keep reading?

ABOUT THE AUTHOR

NANCY PIRRI

Nancy Schumacher is the owner-publisher of Melange Books, LLC, writing under the pseudonyms, Nancy Pirri and Natasha Perry. She is a member of Romance Writers of America. She is also one of the founders of the RWA chapter, Northern Lights Writers (NLW), and is a member of Midwest Fiction Writers and Romancing the Lakes chapters in Minnesota.

www.nancypirri.com

ALSO BY NANCY PIRRI

Montana Women

Katie and the Marshal

Annie and the Outlaw

Janie and the Judge

Laura and the Railroad Baron

Contemporary Romance

Bait Shop Blue

All I Ever Wanted

I Wish You Love, a Spicy Romance Anthology

Make Me Behave (An Anthology) with Tara Fox Hall

Historical Romance

The MacAulay Bride

Featured in the following anthologies:

Romance and Mystery Under the Northern Lights

Western Ways

Food and Romance Go Together, Vol. 2

Writing erotica as Natasha Perry

Ruined Hearts

www.ingramcontent.com/pod-product-compliance
Lightning Source LLC
Chambersburg PA
CBHW020644130626
46552CB00003B/1393